PRAISE FOR MAGGIE SHAYNE

"Ms. Shayne knows just how to tailor the vampire legend to create top-notch romance."
—*Romantic Times* magazine

"Maggie Shayne's WINGS IN THE NIGHT stories offer a challenging mystery draped in the dark folds of vampire love and lore."
—*Gothic Journal*

"Maggie Shayne's writing is excellent, her plotting tremendous, and her characters superb!"
—*Rendezvous*

PRAISE FOR MARILYN TRACY

Winner of the 1990 *Romantic Times* Lifetime Achievement Award for Series Romance for New Romantic Adventure

SOMETHING BEAUTIFUL: Winner of the 1995 *Romantic Times* magazine Award for Best Silhouette Shadows

"…the wonderfully talented Marilyn Tracy… creates searing and passionate magic…"
—*Romantic Times* magazine

Dear Reader,

It's autumn. There's a nip in the air, the light has a special quality it only takes on at this time of year, and soon witches and warlocks (most of them under three feet tall!) will be walking the streets of towns everywhere. And along with them will come vampires, perhaps the most dangerously alluring of all romantic heroes. (The six-foot-tall variety, anyway!) So in honor of the season, this month we're bringing you *Brides of the Night,* a two-in-one collection featuring vampire heroes who are (dare I say it?) to die for. Maggie Shayne continues her wonderful WINGS IN THE NIGHT miniseries with *Twilight Vows,* while Marilyn Tracy lures you in with *Married by Dawn.* Let them wrap you in magic.

We've got more great miniseries going on this month, too. With *Harvard's Education,* Suzanne Brockmann continues her top-selling TALL, DARK AND DANGEROUS miniseries. Readers have been asking for Harvard's story, and now this quintessential tough guy is rewarded with a romance of his own. Then follow our writers out west, as Carla Cassidy begins the saga of MUSTANG, MONTANA, with *Her Counterfeit Husband,* and Margaret Watson returns to CAMERON, UTAH, in *For the Children.* Jill Shalvis, an experienced author making her first appearance here, also knows how great a cowboy hero can be, as she demonstrates in our WAY OUT WEST title, *Hiding Out at the Circle C.* Finally, welcome Hilary Byrnes. This brand-new author is Intimate Moments' WOMAN TO WATCH. And after you read her powerful debut, *Motive, Means...and Marriage?* you *will* be watching—for her next book!

Enjoy! And come back again next month, when we bring you six more of the best and most exciting romance novels around—right here in Silhouette Intimate Moments.

Leslie J. Wainger
Executive Senior Editor

Please address questions and book requests to:
Silhouette Reader Service
U.S.: 3010 Walden Ave., P.O. Box 1325, Buffalo, NY 14269
Canadian: P.O. Box 609, Fort Erie, Ont. L2A 5X3

Brides of the Night

of the Night

MAGGIE SHAYNE
MARILYN TRACY

Silhouette®
INTIMATE™ MOMENTS®

Published by Silhouette Books

America's Publisher of Contemporary Romance

SILHOUETTE BOOKS

ISBN 0-373-07883-8

BRIDES OF THE NIGHT

TWILIGHT VOWS
Copyright © 1998 by Margaret Benson

MARRIED BY DAWN
Copyright © 1998 by Tracy LeCocq

This edition published by arrangement with Harlequin Books S.A.

® and TM are trademarks of Harlequin Books S.A., used under license.
Trademarks indicated with ® are registered in the United States Patent
and Trademark Office, the Canadian Trade Marks Office and in other
countries.

Printed in U.S.A.

CONTENTS

MAGGIE SHAYNE,

a national bestselling author whom *Romantic Times* magazine calls "brilliantly inventive," has written seventeen novels for Silhouette. Her Silhouette single title release, *Born in Twilight* (3/97), was based on her popular vampire series for Shadows, WINGS IN THE NIGHT.

Maggie has won numerous awards, including a *Romantic Times* magazine Career Achievement Award. A three-time finalist for the Romance Writers of America's prestigious RITA Award, Maggie also writes mainstream contemporary fantasy.

In her spare time, Maggie enjoys collecting gemstones, reading tarot cards, hanging out on the Genie computer network and spending time outdoors. She lives in a rural town in central New York with her husband, Rick, five beautiful daughters and a bulldog named Wrinkles. Look for Maggie's next book, *That Mysterious Texas Brand Man,* part of Silhouette Books new World's Most Eligible Bachelors series, in December 1998.

MARILYN TRACY

lives in Portales, New Mexico, in a ramshackle turn-of-the-century house with her son, two dogs, three cats and a poltergeist. Between remodeling the house to its original Victorian-cum-Deco state, writing full-time and finishing a forty-foot cement dragon in the backyard, Marilyn composes full soundtracks to go with each of her novels.

After having lived in both Tel Aviv and Moscow in conjunction with the U.S. State Department, Marilyn enjoys writing about the cultures she's explored and the people she's grown to love. She likes to hear from people who enjoy her books, and always has a pot of coffee on or a glass of wine ready for anyone dropping by, especially if they don't mind the chaos and know how to wield a paintbrush.

TWILIGHT VOWS

Maggie Shayne

Books by Maggie Shayne

Silhouette Intimate Moments

Fortune's Children

Silhouette Shadows

Silhouette Books

Chapter 1

Irish countryside, 1808

I walked along the path that night, as I often did. Bone-tired from working in my father's fields, coated in a layer of good Irish soil spread fine on my skin and held fast by my sweat. My muscles ached, but 'twas a good sort of pain. The sort that came of relishing one's own strength and vigor. Of late, I hadn't done so any too often. I'd been taken with bouts of weakness, my head spinning sometimes until I passed out cold as a corpse. But today hadn't been like that at all. Today I'd felt good, certain whatever had plagued me was gone. And to prove it I'd worked like a horse in Da's fields. All the day through I'd put my brothers and cousins through their paces, darin' them to keep up with me, laughing when they couldn't. And I'd kept on wielding my hoe long after the others had called it a night.

So 'twas alone I was walking.

Autumn hung in the air, with the harvest beneath it and

a big yellow moon hanging low in the sky. Leaves crackled
under my feet and sent their aromas up to meet me as I
walked by the squash patch, with its gray-blue hubbards as
big as Ma's stew pot, and orange-yellow pumpkins clinging
to their dying vines. We'd have to gather them in tomorrow. Gram said there would be a killing frost before next
Sabbath.

A killing frost.

A little chill snaked up the back of my neck as the words
repeated themselves, for some reason, in my mind. Foolishness, of course. I'd spent too many nights as a lad, curled
on a braided rug before the hearth listenin' to Gram spin
her yarns. This time of the year, her tales tended toward
the frightening, with ghosties and ghoulies her favorite sub-
jects. I supposed some of those tales had stuck in my mind.
Though a man grown now, and all of twenty years plus
three, I still got the shivers from Gram's tales. The way her
voice would change as she told 'em, the way her ice-blue
eyes would narrow as if she were sharing some dark secret
while the firelight cast dancing shadows on her dear care-
worn face.

'Twas a night just like this one, boy. When all seemed
peaceful and right. But any fool ought to know better than
to walk alone after dark during the time of the harvest. For
the veil between the world of the living and that of the dead
is thinning...and parting...and...

"Hush, Gram," I whispered. But a chill breeze caressed
my neck and goose bumps rose there to mark its passing.
I thrust my hands into my pockets, hunching my shoulders,
walking a little faster. Something skittered along the road-
side, and my head jerked sharply to the right. "Only the
wind," I said, and then I began to whistle.

Any fool ought to know better. Are you a fool, Donovan
O'Roark?

I shook myself and walked still faster. There were eyes

on me…someone watching from the crisp, black night. Or perhaps some*thing*. A wolf or even an owl. I told myself 'twas nothing, that I'd no reason to fear, but my breath began to hitch in my throat before puffing out in great clouds, and my heart to pound too quickly.

Then the dizziness came.

The ground buckled and heaved before me, though I know it never truly moved at all. I staggered sideways, would have fallen into the weeds along the edge of the path, had I not managed to brace my hand against a nearby tree. Palm flat to the warm, soft trunk, head hanging low, I fought to catch my breath, to cling to my consciousness.

The tree spoke.

"Alas, boy, I thought to wait…but I can see the deed must be done tonight."

I jerked my head up, then snatched my hand away, not from a tree, but from a man. Yet…not a man. His dark eyes swirled with the endless black of the very night, and his hair was black as soot, gleaming to midnight blue where the moon's rays alighted. His lips, cherry red, and full. Yet the pallor of his skin shocked me. Not sickly-looking, not like death. But fair, and fine, as if he were some fine work of art chiseled of pale granite. As if he were a part of the moonlight itself.

I took a step backward, leaves crunching, the breeze picking up to tease my hair. The wind grew stronger all of a sudden…almost as if it knew something dire was about to take place this autumn night…

…*the veil between the world of the living and the world of the dead is thinning…parting…*

I backed away more quickly.

The creature only shook his head.

"Don't try to run. It will do you no good."

"Who are you?" I managed. "What do you want with me?"

His smile was sad, bitter. "Many things, Donovan. Many things. But for now...just the one." He reached out, though I never saw his hands move. They were simply there before him one moment, moving expressively as he spoke—and in the next instant they clasped the front of my homespun shirt. I struggled against him, but he pulled me easily to him, and my fighting amounted to nothing at all.

I am not a small man, nor a weak one, despite my recent illness. I stood fully a head taller than my da, and half that much above any other man in our village. My shoulders were broad and well formed by a lifetime of hard work. I'd never met a man I wasn't certain I could whip, should the need arise.

Yet this one, this *thing,* dragged me to him as if I were a child. Closer, inexorably closer, even as I twisted and tugged and fought for my freedom. He bent over me. Fear clutched at my heart, nearly stopping its frantic beat. Pain shot out through my chest, and down my left arm, and I couldn't draw air into my lungs.

Then I felt his mouth on my neck...lips parting, and the shocking pain as his teeth sank deeply into the skin of my throat, piercing me. Pain that faded almost as quickly as it appeared. And as it faded, so did everything else. Everything around me, from the soft singing of the crickets to the smell of the decaying leaves. I no longer felt the chill autumn air. There were three things of which I remained aware, three things that filled all my senses. Darkness. Silence. And the feel of his mouth on my throat, draining the very life from me.

Then even those things disappeared.

"Donovan! Donny-boy, wake up! Wake up!"

Someone shook my shoulders. Da's voice shouted in my ears, sounding like it never had. Raspy, panicky, afraid. There was a taste in my mouth, salty and rich. I wiped my lips with the back of my hand, as I fought to open my eyes. When I looked at my hand, I saw blood, glittering in the moonlight.

What had I done? What…?

Da scooped me up into old arms that shouldn't have had the strength to lift me. And staggering under my weight, he carried me toward the village, shouting for help. It was only moments before others came, my neighbors, my friends. Alicia with her flowing auburn curls and cat's eyes as green as Ireland itself, the girl I dreamed about at night. My ma, and sisters. My body was jostled as neighbor men relieved Da of the burden, and bore me swiftly into my home. They lowered me to a pallet, while Ma shouted questions. But no one could answer her. No one knew what had befallen me out there on the path this night. Only me, and one other soul. A monster, a creature of nightmares and Gram's tales.

Gram. Gram would know what had happened, what this meant. I listened for her voice among the others, but it was a long while before I heard it. And its grimness did nothing to reassure me.

"It can only be evil," she all but whispered. "'Tis the Eve of All Hallows. Foolish lad, out walking alone tonight of all nights!"

Ma hushed her impatiently, but I saw the way she stiffened at Gram's words. She snatched up a lamp, elbowing the men aside and leaning over me as if to see for herself. Then Ma gasped and drew slightly away, her loving eyes going wider.

"Lord a' mercy, there be blood on his lips."

"Aye," Da said. "But what does it mean?"

My mother said nothing. Gently, her hands pushed my shirt aside as she searched for injuries. I forced my eyes to remain open, though sleep…

Or is that death?

...called to me, drew me closer just as the stranger had done. I couldn't fight much longer.

Ma looked down at me, fear growing large in her eyes, though I could see her trying to keep it concealed from me. "You'll be all right, my boy. I'll see to that. You'll be—"

As she spoke, she pushed my hair aside. 'Twas long, my hair. Hung well past my shoulders, thick and darkest brown. My Ma lifted the heavy locks, and her eyes changed.

As if the light of love flickered...a guttering candle.

She snatched up a cloth, muttering a prayer in the old language as she dabbed the blood away from my throat with one hand and lifted her lamp higher with the other.

And then my mother screamed. "Devil! Demon spawn! Get the children out of this house, 'tis the mark of Satan!"

I felt my eyes widen as her face turned hateful. I lifted a hand toward her as she backed away. "Ma, what's wrong with you? 'Tis me, your son, Donovan—"

But she shook her head, her eyes fixed to the place on my throat where that creature had feasted, and she continued to back away. "Die, Lucifer," she whispered to me. Her son, her firstborn. And I couldn't believe she said it, couldn't believe the hatred in her eyes. "You're not my son, nor worthy to be there in his poor body. Die, or I vow I'll kill you myself."

I'd been fighting to hold on. But her words...the shock they sent through my body...'twas all it took to shake my tenuous grip on life. And I sank into darkness. Into death.

This time, the darkness lasted longer, though I was never aware of the passing of time. I only knew I felt clean when I began to surface toward life once more. My body, my clothing...were fresh. I smelled of heather and honeysuckle. The clothes I wore were not the scratchy, rough weave I wore every day, either. Ma had dressed me in a fine suit of clothes she'd made for me herself, and only allowed me to wear on the most important occasions.

I heard voices, smelled the familiar scent of tallow candles and lamps. And flowers. So many flowers. Someone played a fiddle, drawing the bow 'cross the strings in a slow and mournful wail. I heard the clink of glasses, and smelled good beer, and food.

Slowly, I managed to get my eyes open.

I never should have done that. For I found that I lay in a coffin. Homemade, likely by my da's own hand. The coffin had been set upon a table at O'Connor's tavern. Women walked past, heads low, tears damp on their cheeks. Men stood still, drinking beer from tin tankards. Sean Ryan stood in a corner with his fiddle tucked under his chin, eyes closed. Alicia, the girl I'd often kissed when her da wasn't looking, sat by herself in a chair, staring straight ahead, but seeing nothing.

Father Murphy stood up front, right beside the coffin, his back to me, his prayer book opened, and by clearing his throat he got everyone to look his way.

"Donovan O'Roark was a good man, but evil struck him down in the prime of his youth…"

Lord a' mercy, they were givin' me a funeral!

"No, Father," I cried as loud as I could manage. "I'm alive…Da, Ma, I'm…" I struggled to sit up.

Someone screamed, and then the room went dead silent. Father Murphy faced me, white as a specter, wide-eyed as he crossed himself. Alicia leapt to her feet and shouted, "Kill it! Kill it before it destroys us all!"

"No!" I cried. "I'm not evil! 'Tis me, Donovan O'Roark…won't someone listen…?"

"Get the women and children out," Father Murphy shouted, and for the first time I thought he sounded like some mighty prophet of old. His voice fairly shook the walls. Or perhaps 'twas my hearing that was altered, for indeed it seemed every voice was sharper, clearer to me. And the fiddle…

No time to dwell on that now, for my best friend Sean and some of the other young men began urging the women out of the tavern.

My ma stayed behind, glancing at me, then at my da. "You know what must be done."

Da nodded, and Ma fairly ran from the room then.

I braced my hands on the sides of the coffin, making as if to get myself out, thinking how they'd all laugh once they realized how foolish they were being, and—

Da shoved me back. Hard. Cruel. Never had he handled me so roughly. I blinked in shock. Then froze—literally felt the ice creeping through my veins—as I saw Father Murphy take a wooden stake from somewhere nearby, muttering, "Your wife was right, O'Roark. 'Tis good we were prepared for this." He pressed the tip of the stake to my chest, and my da, *my own beloved da,* handed him the mallet.

From outside I could hear my mother sobbing softly and the girl I planned to marry one day shouting "Kill it! Kill it *now!*"

Father Murphy lifted the mallet.

I don't know where the strength came from—or, I didn't know then. I suppose I blamed it on panic or fear, rather than anything preternatural. But when I shoved against the hands that held me—my father's hands—I felt little resistance. I surged from that coffin with the force of a tidal wave, and landed on my feet beyond the two of them. My trusted confessor and my flesh-and-blood sire. My would-be executioners.

"Da, how can you do this? What have I done to deserve—"

"He's not your son," Father Murphy said. "He's evil, the same evil that took your son away. Do not heed him."

"But I *am* your son! Da, look at me!"

Da turned away. "Get thee behind me, Satan."

"Da, 'tis me, your firstborn..."

He faced me again with blood in his eyes. Yanking the stake and mallet from the priest's hands, my father surged at me, and suddenly there was no doubt in my mind he meant to do murder. I spun away and ran. Out the front door, the only door, and right through the midst of that crowd of mourners who'd called themselves my friends. My family. My woman.

"Get it!" someone cried. "It mustn't escape!"

And I fled. Shoving them aside easily, I ran, faster than I'd known I could run. I heard the pursuit. Some had fetched dogs, others had mounted their horses. I saw the flickering of yellow-orange torchlight coming closer as I ran for my very life. And they kept coming.

Someone yanked me off my feet and into the bushes alongside the path. I looked up, and saw the creature who'd brought all of this upon me, and I opened my mouth to curse his very existence. He easily covered it, stilling me and drawing me deep into the cover of the greenery. A second later the mob thundered past, shouting and cursing me, promising to destroy me in the most horrible ways imaginable. Calling me "Satan."

My captor no longer needed to hold me still, for I had no will to move. I relaxed to the ground, lowering my head as tears burned my eyes. My pursuers were gone. My assassin remained, but I no longer cared. "Kill me if you will," I offered. "I've no reason to wish to live."

"You have it all wrong, Donovan," he told me, and gripping my arms, he pulled me to my feet. Strong hands, gripping me hard, but no pain as a result. "You were dying before. The weakness, the dizziness, the blackouts."

I looked up sharply.

"Oh, yes, I've been watching you. You'd have been

dead within a few more days, at most. But you…you didn't want death." He lowered his head, shook it. "Rarely have I come upon a man as vividly alive and in love with life as you, my friend."

I frowned, shook my head. "Then why did you try to kill me?"

"I wasn't trying to kill you, Donovan. I was giving you life. You'll never die now. You can't."

"I…I can't…?"

"Well, there are ways, but…listen to me, lad. I took your blood, drained you to the point of death. And then I fed you from my own veins and filled you once again. It's how the dark gift is shared, how it's given."

"Dark gift. I don't know—"

"Immortality," he told me.

I stood there, blinking in confusion and staring up at this man. His dark head silhouetted by a Halloween moon, and bordered by the clawlike, leafless branches of slumbering trees. A pumpkin patch at his back. An owl singing of my death in the distance. And I think I sensed then, finally, just what he was about to say.

"My name is Dante, and I am a vampire."

I gasped, but he took my hand in a firm grip and shook it.

"Your name is Donovan," he told me, patient as if he were a teacher instructing a slow student. "And as of tonight, you are a vampire, too."

Chapter 2

Rachel Sullivan waltzed into O'Mallory's pub as if she'd never been gone, and ignored the hush that fell as she passed. Glasses stopped clinking, men stopped spinning their yarns. Eyes followed her when she sashayed to the back of the room and snatched a white apron from a hook. Behind the gleaming mahogany bar, Mary folded her arms over her plump middle and smiled. Rachel tied the apron on and turned around, eyeing the round, wooden tables and the familiar faces at each one.

"An' what's got you all so tongue-tied?" she asked, tossing her head. "I told you I'd come back, and now I have. So stop your gaping and drink your ale." She turned briskly back to the bar, snatching up a tray with two foaming pints on it, and then unerringly spotted the pair who had empty glasses before them, and delivered their refills.

The talk started up again. Mostly directed at her now. Unshaven men who'd known her father, welcoming her home. Curly-headed women asking her about the States as she hustled back and forth with her laden tray. For the first time in what seemed like a long time, Rachel released a long, cleansing breath, and felt the tension drain from her spine. She was home, truly home. And it felt good. Better than the degree she'd worked so hard to earn. Better than anything had since…since before she'd left.

She'd been afraid, half expecting the locals to be wary of her now, but the rapid return to normalcy in the pub told her that fear had been unwarranted. The people of Dunkinny didn't like outsiders, that much was true. Oh, tourists occasionally found their way to the isolated village, particularly the ones with Irish surnames out to discover their roots. The locals were polite enough, but always reserved. Wary. Rachel, though, had been born and raised here. Orphaned here, and taken under the collective wing of these villagers. They'd been sad when she'd left them, but not angry. With one exception—Marney Neal, who'd been so determined to marry her. But he wasn't here tonight, she noted with relief. And the others welcomed her back into their midst without a second thought. Eight years away, but they didn't see her as an outsider.

"Welcome home, Rachel." Mary, who'd owned this place and the boarding house attached to it for as long as Rachel could remember, hugged her hard, slapping her back with enthusiastic blows. "I've kept your old room for you. I can already see you'll be takin' your old job back."

Rachel didn't have the heart to tell her it was only for a short time. Only until she got her thesis written, the final step in earning her doctorate. And then she'd…

What? Become the world's leading social anthropologist? Teach at an Ivy League university in the States?

She closed her eyes and inhaled the scent of Russell Finnegan's stale pipe smoke, fresh beer, and the sheep manure on Mitch Marley's boots. When she opened them again, she faced the window, and stared out at the worn track that passed for a road in this tiny village, and the rolling emerald hills, and the crumbling castle—Castle Dante—in the distance. It stood amid a ghostly mist as haunting as the tale that went along with the place—the tale she was basing her thesis on. Beyond the castle were the cliffs, and the green-blue sea far below.

And that was the other reason she'd come back. To see that castle one more time.

As a child, she'd believed in the tales. But in her heart, she'd never accepted the villagers' condemnation of the men who'd once lived there. One of them, she swore, had come to her. Twice in her childhood she'd met him, or so she'd believed for a long time. The first time had been when she'd nearly drowned in the river one night long ago. A dark stranger had pulled her from the water, breathed into her lungs, cradled her gently until others arrived, and then disappeared before she'd even had a chance to thank him. The second time was after her parents' deaths, when she'd lain awake and afraid in her bed, unable to sleep, feeling more alone than any being ever had. He'd come to her, held her hand, and told her she wasn't alone at all. That she had a guardian who would watch over her, protect her always, and that she must never fear. She'd barely seen his face in the darkness, but in her mind, she'd believed him to be Donovan O'Roark, or his ghost. And she'd loved him.

Always, she'd loved him. Even later, when she'd realized her childhood memories were only dreams, and that there were no such things as vampires, she'd nurtured a tender place for the fictional legend in her heart. And while she was home, she'd visit that castle once more…perhaps just to assure herself that he wasn't truly there, awaiting her return.

She'd been home for two weeks when he came.

The air was brisk, with the cold taste of winter on its

lips when it kissed her face. But the doors of the pub were propped open all the same, to let the pipe smoke out and the fresh air in. And the fire snapping in Mary's cobblestone hearth kept the chill at bay.

When the silence fell this time, it was uneasy, rather than the friendly hush that had fallen upon Rachel's unexpected return. Then, she'd felt the smiling eyes, the welcome. Now she felt a frisson of something icy slipping up her spine. And when she turned to follow the curious gazes, she saw the stranger walking along the darkened road.

He paused, and stared off in the distance, toward the dark hulking silhouette of the castle. Mitch Marley gasped. Russell Finnegan gaped and his pipe dropped from his lax mouth to the table, unnoticed.

The tension that filled the room, filled *her,* was ridiculous, and unnecessary. "I'd forgot," she muttered, "just how superstitious you all are. Look at you, gawking at that fellow as if he's Donovan O'Roark come back from the dead!"

Mary crossed herself. "You saying you don't believe the old tales now that you're educated, Rachel Sullivan?"

"Old tales are just that. Old tales. Nothing more. I'll prove it, too." Rachel stepped into the open doorway, hands braced on either side, and leaned out. "I don't know where you're going, stranger, but if it's food and a warm bed you're lookin' for, you won't find it anywhere but here."

"Lord preserve us from that saucy girl," Mary murmured.

"Feisty as she ever was," someone agreed.

But Rachel ignored them, because the man was turning, looking at her. It was dark tonight, no moon to help her explore his face. She could only see dark eyes gleaming the reflection of the soft, muted light spilling out of the pub. Firelight and lamp glow. Mary detested bright electric lights at nighttime, though Rachel often suspected it was the bill she truly disliked.

"Come inside," Rachel said again, more softly this time because she sensed he could hear her very well. "Warm yourself by the fire. And show these friends of mine that you're not the monster from their favorite folktale."

I stood there, stunned to my bones. Amazed first that she'd spoken to me at all, for I knew the people of Dunkinny to be a superstitious lot, untrusting of strangers. Or they had been when I'd first left here, nigh on a hundred years ago, and they had been so still each time I'd returned since. But people in solitary villages like this one never tend to change overmuch. She was different, though. She'd always been different.

I fancied it ironic; I'd been one of them once, and that wariness, that mistrust of strangers, was still with me. But I'd been betrayed too often to let it go. It was, in fact, stronger than ever.

So then, why did I stop? Why did I turn and look at her when she spoke to me, when my natural reaction would have been to keep walking, never so much as pausing in my gait.

But I did pause. Partly because of her voice, pure and silken, with the lilt of Ireland, of this very village to it. So familiar and dear to me, that accent. And frightening at the same time. 'Twas the voice of my own people, the ones who'd called me evil and tried to kill me. The ones who'd later murdered the best friend I'd ever had. But 'twas also the voice of the little girl I'd watched over long ago, but grown up now. And somehow, still the same.

She spoke again, her tone haughty, mischievous, almost taunting. And then I looked, and saw her silhouetted in the doorway, surrounded by a golden glow. Raven hair, long and wild. I'd seen Gypsies less mesmerizing.

She held out a hand to me. "Come," she said.

And as if her words held some sort of power over me, I went.

She clasped my hand as soon as I came within reach, and she drew me inside. She had long sharp nails. Red nails. I liked them, and the warmth of her small, strong hand. And the tingle of sensual awareness I felt passing through her body. I liked that, too. Knew better than to indulge it this close to what would soon be my home... again. But liked it all the same.

Over the years, I had changed, but not drastically. My skin was paler, yes. It hadn't felt the touch of the sun in nearly two centuries, after all. But its pink, healthy glow remained intact for several hours once I'd fed.

And I'd fed well tonight.

So when she drew me inside, there were no gasps of shock at my appearance. She settled me into a wooden chair near the fire, and that's when I realized this pub was in the exact place that other one had stood long ago. O'Connor's tavern. The site of my funeral. The place where my father had tried to murder me.

A lump came into my throat, but I forced it away.

"There, you see?" the girl was saying, hands on her hips, which moved enticingly whenever she did. She waved a hand toward me. "Just a tourist, not a legend come to life." She faced me again. "Tell us, stranger, what's your name?"

I cleared my throat. "O'Roark," I said, waiting, curious to see their reactions.

The plump woman dropped a tankard of ale and it crashed to the floor, spewing amber liquid and odorous foam around her feet.

The girl stared at me, searching my face with an intensity

that shook me. But she couldn't recognize me. She'd never seen my face clearly enough to know it again now. And finally she grinned, a twinkle in her eye, and tilted her head to one side. "O'Roark, is it? Another one? Tell me, Mr. O'Roark, have you come travelin' from the States in search of your family history?"

I smiled very slightly, unable to help myself. Such a spirited girl, she was. "Has my accent faded so much that I sound like an American to you?" I asked her.

She gave me a sassy shrug. "I only know you're not from Dunkinny. For I know everyone in this town."

"You've lived here that long, have you?"

"Born here, as were my parents and theirs before them for five generations."

"Mine, too."

She frowned at me, and I took my time studying her face. Small features, fine bones. But her lips were full and her eyes large in that small face. "You're saying you're descended from *our* O'Roarks?"

"So much so that I've inherited the castle."

At last, I'd shaken her. The others had been uneasy from the moment I'd set foot inside, but not her. Now, though, I saw it. The widening of her deep green eyes, the loss of blood's glow in her cheeks.

"You're making it up," she accused, but softly.

I shook my head.

"He'll be wantin' to know about the legend then," Mary called.

"Aye, tell him the legend, Rachel! Stranger he may be, but no man ought to risk dallying about that place un-warned."

Rachel. She'd grown into the name. A name as untamed and tempting as the woman she'd become.

She tilted her head to one side. "He already knows," she ventured, studying me, watching my every reaction.

"How can you be sure?" I asked her. "Tell me, Rachel. What is this legend that seems to make everyone here so nervous? Everyone…but you, that is."

She recovered quickly, regaining the bounce in her step as she snatched two steins of ale from the bar, and brought them to the table. One, she thumped to the table before me. The other, she drank from deeply, before wiping her mouth with the back of her hand and leaning back in the chair she'd taken.

Behind her the fire snapped and danced. "Long ago Donovan O'Roark, a farmer's son loved by all, was walking home from the fields. Alone, he walked, and well after dark, on the Eve of All Hallows."

I got a chill up my spine, and was reminded, briefly and vividly of my gram, and the way she'd spun her tales before the fire at night. Tales I'd never believed in.

"But poor Donovan never made it home unscathed that night, for a creature attacked him." She paused, looking around the room. I did likewise, seeing the rapt attention on every face—though they'd likely all heard the tale a hundred times by now. "A vampire," she said in a long, whispery breath.

I lifted my brows high, an attempt to show them my skepticism. "A vampire," I repeated.

"Indeed. The young man died that night, but he didn't stay dead long. He rose from his casket at his own funeral! No longer mortal, but a creature like the one who'd created him. The villagers tried to kill him, but he was too strong, and he escaped into the night and vanished."

I lifted the mug to my mouth, pretending to sip the beer, and licking the taste of it from my lips when I set the glass down again. "I still don't see what this has to do with the castle."

"Ah, so you're an impatient one, are you?"

I only shrugged and let her continue.

"Donovan wasn't seen again. Not for a hundred years. But everyone knew his tale. Then, something happened. The lord of that castle," here she pointed in the castle's general direction, "was a rich Italian man, some said a nobleman. His name was Dante. Now how do you suppose his castle ended up in the hands of the family O'Roark?" I smiled and said nothing. Rachel went on. "No one had ever suspected Dante of anything evil. He simply kept to himself, and that was the way the villagers liked it."

"He being an outsider, and all," I put in.

She gave me a curious glance. "One night a young girl, who'd been hired to work sometimes at the castle, came running down from the cliffs, hysterical. Screaming and crying, she was. With blood runnin' down her neck in twin streams, and two tiny punctures in her pretty throat."

I didn't interrupt her, though the words near choked me trying to escape. Dante had never harmed the girl. He'd adored her, loved her to distraction, and in the end, done the one thing he'd warned me over and over never to do.

He'd trusted her.

Rachel sipped her beer. "The girl said Dante was a monster who slept in a coffin by day, and fed on livin' blood by night. He'd attacked her, tried to drain her dry, but she'd got away."

"Did anyone wonder," I asked, unable to keep still any longer, "how a young thing like that could get away from a creature like him?"

She frowned at me. "You want to hear the rest or not?"

I nodded. She spoke. "The girl said Dante wasn't alone up there. She said he had another with him, and that companion was none other than Donovan O'Roark."

Around the room everyone nodded, muttering in agreement.

"The villagers discussed what needed to be done, while young Laura begged them to destroy the monsters. Finally, they agreed. At just before dawn they marched to the castle armed with torches and oil, and they set the place alight." When she said it, I thought she suppressed a shudder.

I remembered it all too well. The flames, the sickening realization that the woman Dante had loved had betrayed him in the worst possible way. His pained expression as he realized it, too. I knew that pain so well, because I'd felt it when my own family, and the girl I'd loved, had done the same to me.

"The vampires were forced to flee, and when they did, the sun was already coming up. And the castle has been owned by an O'Roark ever since." She stopped. I felt her hand on my arm. "Mister O'Roark?"

I opened my eyes, just realizing I had squeezed them shut.

"Are you all right?"

"It…it's a frightening tale. Gruesome."

"But just a tale, as I've been trying to tell these good people."

I nodded. "Go on, finish it. What became of the two victims?"

She tilted her head. "Victims?" Lowering her gaze, her voice softer, she said, "I never thought anyone else would see them that way. But you're right, 'tis exactly what they were." She met my eyes again, her voice more normal. "At any rate, they ran off in separate directions, but smoke could be seen curling from their clothes as they went. The villagers believed they both died, burned to cinders by the sun." She shook her head, almost sadly. "But not long after that, a crew of men arrived to begin working on the castle, and when they were questioned they would only say a man named O'Roark had hired them. The villagers believed it was Donovan, back from the dead a second time. They all said he'd return one day to seek vengeance on the people of Dunkinny for the murder of his friend."

She sighed deeply, and for a long moment no one spoke, still under the spell of her story. But Rachel broke the silence a moment later. "I'm sure most of the locals are speculating as to whether you be him. Tell them your given name, O'Roark. Ease their superstitious minds."

I smiled very gently, and laid money on the table to pay for my unfinished beer. Then got to my feet and turned for the door. "My given name," I said softly, "is Donovan." And then I stepped into the night, away from all of them and the dread on their faces.

Chapter 3

Someone was following me.

I slowed my pace slightly, keeping to the shadows, moving in utter silence. My mind open, probing, tracking the curious fool. Only one. No threat to me.

I never should've done it; taunted them the way I did. I knew better, and to this day I've no idea what possessed me to tell them my name, watch them go pale, and then walk away. I'd frightened the fools, deliberately frightened them. But it was no less than they deserved. They'd built themselves up a hefty debt over the generations. Turning on one of their own the way they'd turned on me so long ago. Murdering Dante...

I paused along the roadside where the heather bloomed its last and its scent was heavy in the air, lowered my head as the pain swept over me along with the autumn wind. They'd surrounded the castle, and brutally put their torches to our home, our sanctuary, forcing us to run for our lives. But we'd only found the rising sun awaiting our desperate flight. Its golden rays, so beautiful, so deadly. I remember the searing, the blistering of my flesh, the horror that surged within me as I saw thin tendrils of smoke rising up from my own body.

I'd been the lucky one that cold morn. By burrowing deep into a haystack in a field—a field I'd once worked at my father's side—I found shelter. But for Dante…I knew him to be dead. For I never saw him again after that day, and I've no doubt he'd have contacted me somehow if he'd survived.

Lifting my head, I sent my senses out, realizing that in the flood of memories this place evoked, I'd lost track of my follower.

But the stalker had stopped as well, and stood now several yards away, just watching, and thinking herself protected by the darkness. I almost smiled at her innocence, turned, and began walking again, wondering how far her courage would take her.

I'd left this place after the attack. Traveled, saw the world, lived in so many places I barely remember them all. But of people, of others like myself and mortals the same, I saw little. I can list the name of every person I've ever had words with in the past two hundred years, and that's how few they've been.

Dante drilled it into me, again and again. "Trust no one, Donovan. No one. And most especially, no mortal."

I could hear the sea in the distance now, and the road ran away from the farmers' fields and began to slope sharply upward, among rises too steep, and far too rocky, to be tilled. She was still following.

So long as we'd lived by Dante's words, we'd been fine. A lonely life, it was. But safe, peaceful. Satisfying in so many other ways. The time we had, endless time—or so we believed then—to learn of music and art, to read and to write, to experience and to savor the things our mortal lifetimes would never have given us time to know.

But then Dante had fallen in love, and it had all ended. He'd told the girl the truth, and it seemed to me she must have run all the way back to that ignorant mass of villagers, so eager was she to tell our secret and see us destroyed.

Dante had been right from the start. Trust no one, and particularly, no mortal.

As I crested the hill, the wind blew in from the sea more fiercely, and I loved the feel of it. My wind, my sea. So familiar despite the bitterness I'd known here. I sat down amid a small outcropping of boulders along the road-side...not because I was tired.

The castle towered before me, no sign of the fire that had nearly killed me a century ago. Dante had willed the place to me, and I'd had it restored, or partially so. I kept it up, always, ready for his return. I'd long ago given up hope he'd ever come back...but somehow I couldn't let go of this place.

My good friend was gone, and I was alone in the world. There was no room to doubt that. And yet some foolish sentimental urge had drawn me back here to the very place where he'd been brutally murdered. Back to this place, to the castle, to my ancestral home—to her. I'd been drawn to see her again, to assure myself she was still safe and well.

She was nearly upon me now, the wind whipping her hair into wild chaos. Her eyes narrowing as she squinted into the darkness, trying to see where I'd gone. She thought she was stepping lightly, but I heard every footfall. Not that it would have mattered. She had a scent about her, one that was sharply different from the others—from any other mortal I'd encountered. Dante had told me that some did, and he'd told me what it meant.

Among other things, *vital* things, it meant that I was

forbidden to harm her. By whose decree, I never knew. Never asked. Besides, I never was much for rules. But I couldn't have harmed her if I'd tried.

She came closer. Her long skirt snapped in the sea wind, whipping her ankles. Her blouse…sinfully snug-fitting, and molding to her breasts as if trying to squeeze them. She stood there a moment, so close I could feel her there. And after a fruitless search for me, she lowered her head in defeat. But still she remained, letting the wind buffet her body, and I do believe she was thoroughly enjoying its vicious embrace. But then she turned to go.

I stood slowly, silently. "Are you looking for someone?"

She sucked in a loud, violent gasp, spinning toward me, her hands flying to her chest as if to keep her heart from leaping out. Then she paused, blinking at me in the darkness, drawing several openmouthed breaths. "Lordy, you near scared the life out of me!"

I smiled then. Her accent was no longer as pronounced as it used to be, and I knew that was because she'd been away for a time. But it remained enchanting to me. My own had faded until it was barely discernible anymore.

"I was beginning to think," I told her, "that nothing frightened you."

She gave a tilt of her head and a shrug. "Well, it takes a good deal more than an old folktale and a stranger showin' up in the village, claimin' to be a ghost."

"I never claimed to be a ghost."

"You said you were Donovan O'Roark."

"Because I am."

She narrowed her emerald eyes on me. She had witch's eyes, Rachel Sullivan did. "Can you prove it?"

My gaze dipped to the pale, slender column of her throat, and impulsively, I put my fingers there and felt the blood churning beneath her skin. "I could…"

Her eyes sparkled. It was true, nothing frightened her. She smiled at me, and it took my breath away. "Goin' to bite my neck, are you?" she asked.

"If I did, would you run screaming to the villagers, and return with a mob bent on doing me in?"

Tipping her head back, she laughed softly, a deep husky sound. Her neck…so close, so smooth…

She brought her gaze level with mine, obviously amused. "I'd be more likely to bite you back, Donovan O'Roark, and don't you forget it."

I could say nothing. She robbed me of words, of the power of speech, of coherent thought, with that flippant reply.

"But the proof I had in mind," she went on, "was running more along the lines of paperwork. A driver's license, you know, or something of that sort."

Swallowing hard, I retrieved my wallet from my back pocket, extracted my identification and showed it to her. A man in my position did well to keep things such as these up-to-date, and there were many ways of doing so, none too complex. She took it, her fingers brushing mine, perhaps deliberately. She had to squint and finally pulled a cigarette lighter from her deep pocket and, turning her back to the wind, used it to see by.

Nodding sagely, she handed it back to me. "So you really are a descendant—named for your most infamous ancestor, no less." She bit her lower lip. "Is this your first visit to Dunkinny, then?"

She asked it as if trying to hide the question's importance to her. I thought it best not to answer. "Why were you following me, Rachel—it is Rachel, isn't it?"

"Indeed, Rachel Sullivan, with a few notorious ancestors of my own."

The back of my neck prickled to life at the mention of

her ancestors. Treacherous women, women I'd known too well.

She went on. "The Sullivan women are somewhat known for scandals. Perhaps I ought to warn you of that right off. 'Twas one of my own who four generations ago screamed accusations against Lord Dante, and got him killed, or so the legends have it."

It was true, Laura Sullivan had been her name. My throat went dry.

"An' they say another Sullivan woman was promised to marry Donovan O'Roark himself—the first one, that is. But when he rose from his coffin, she cried for his blood."

"Yes," I said softly, hearing her shrill voice again in my mind, shouting, *"Kill it! Kill it before it destroys us all!"* "Alicia," I muttered.

"Really? I never heard her given name before."

I only shrugged. "So have you come to pick up where your forebears left off, Rachel? To destroy me?"

She slipped her arm through mine, and turned us toward the castle, walking slowly. "You're a funny man, Donovan. But you know as well as I those are only silly tales. No truth to 'em, or at least, so little 'tis barely recognizable anymore. No, I have a far different mission. But I'll be needin' your help."

"My help?" She had my curiosity piqued. And yet I feared her. It was too uncanny to be mere coincidence, and a shiver worked up my spine as I wondered if perhaps it was the destiny of the Sullivan women to destroy me—if they'd keep coming, generation after generation of them—until they saw the task completed.

And now I was thinking as foolishly and superstitiously as my people.

"Tell me of this mission, then. What is it?"

She looked up at me and smiled, eyes wide and green

as the sea, full of innocence and mischief like the eyes of the child I remembered.

"I've come to learn all your secrets, Donovan. All the secrets of Castle Dante, and the truth behind the legend."

My heart tripped to a stop in my chest. My voice hoarse, I said, "If I told you all of that, pretty Rachel, I'm afraid I'd have to kill you."

Pressing closer to my side, clapping her hand to my arm and leaning her head on my shoulder, she laughed. A husky, deep sound, genuine amusement ringing in its voice. "I do love a man with a sense of humor," she said. "I can tell we're going to get along, Donovan. Why, we'll be best friends 'fore we're done."

She was warm at my side, and far too close to me. And I relished her nearness…for the lack of human companionship wears a man down over the years.

She was here to destroy me. I had no doubt of that. And yet I couldn't bring myself to send her away. She couldn't force me to tell her anything, I told myself. She couldn't learn anything I didn't wish her to know. What harm would it do to let her accompany me to the castle?

Inside me, I heard Dante's dire warnings: *Don't do it, Donovan. Don't spend another second with her. She's dangerous! She's a Sullivan, dammit. Send her away, or kill her now and be done with it.*

We stopped, the wind blocked now by the towering mass of the castle itself. Before us two massive doors made of broad beams, and held together by black iron bands, stood like sentries awaiting the password.

"Ever since I was a little girl, I've wanted to see inside this castle," she said, so softly it was as if she were that little girl again, right now. "But my parents forbade it, and filled my head with so many foolish old tales that for a time I was frightened to death of sneaking up here the way the older ones did."

"For a time?"

"Aye. Later I changed my mind. He was no monster, the man who lived here. I crept around this place often, once I'd made up my mind to that. So childish, hopin' for a glimpse of a man long dead."

"But you didn't go inside?"

"I couldn't. I always felt…" She drew a deep breath, let it out all at once. "You'll laugh at me."

"No," I said. "I won't. Tell me."

She looked up, right into my eyes, and hers were honest, sincere, beautiful. "I always thought this place seemed… sacred, somehow. And…and it was my own blood kin that defiled it, ruined it. So to me, my setting foot inside would have been…a sacrilege."

"And now?"

She eyed the castle doors, shivered a little. "Maybe I was wrong. Maybe I'm the one who'll make it all right again, somehow." She lowered her head, sighing. "I'm different from the others, you know."

"Yes, I know."

"They tell the tale, again and again, and they all shudder with fear of the creatures they claim lived here once." She placed a palm against the chiseled stone, closed her eyes. "But not me. The first time I heard the tale I was all of three years old, and I cried. For hours, no one could comfort me. To me, it wasn't a horror story, it was a tragedy. One man, rising from the dead only to be driven out of the village by his own family. Another, murdered only because he dared to love." She met my eyes and smiled. "To tell you the truth, back when I was still child enough to believe in the old tales, I thought of your ancestor as…as a friend. My own guardian angel."

"And now?" I asked her.

"And now I'm an adult, who knows better than to believe in fairy tales. But it does seem like Providence that you're here now. Just when I've returned home from the States. Just when I'm planning to write my thesis based on the legend, its sources, and its effects on the community to this day. Just when I'm wondering how I'll ever learn all I need to know about Castle Dante and the original Donovan O'Roark—here you are. I think it's a sign.''

She was enchanting me, mesmerizing me. Both with her scent, and with her beauty, but mostly with that enthusiasm and charm and slightly skewed view of the universe.

She had the belladonna antigen, and that was part of the attraction—had always been drawing me to her, urging me to watch over her. I could smell it in her blood, could sense it there. Every immortal had that antigen before they received the dark gift. If not, they wouldn't transform…they'd simply die. Dante had told me these things, and he'd warned me as well of the allure mortals with the antigen had for us…the attraction. And it was said to run both ways.

I knew all this. But knowing it did nothing to dampen its effect on me. As a child she'd been harmless, no threat to me at all, just a little girl in need of a protector. But now…

She stared up at me from emerald green eyes. ''Will you take me inside, Donovan? With you fulfill my childhood dreams and show me your castle?''

And like a man held prisoner by a Gypsy enchantress's spell, I nodded, searched for my key, and opened my haven up to my enemy.

Chapter 4

There was something about him...

No, it was only her imagination playing games with her. Yes, he was pale, but only slightly so. And that grace about him, the way his every movement seemed as fluid as a part of a dance...it was simply his way. It didn't mean a thing.

He wasn't the guardian of her imagination. Her savior.

He gripped the iron ring and opened the doors, waiting and allowing her to enter first. Taking a single step into the looming, echoing blackness, she stopped, battling a shiver of unease that kept tickling at her spine.

"I can't see a thing," she said, reaching into her pocket for the lighter once again.

She felt him enter behind her. He stood close to her back as she fumbled in her pocket, and the deep moan of the door closing behind him made her heart skip a beat. Closing her hand around the lighter in her pocket, she pulled it out and promptly dropped it on the floor.

"It's all right," he said. "Wait here."

"As if I could do anything else," she replied, and hoped he didn't detect the tremor in her voice.

He moved past her then. She never heard his footsteps, and it seemed they should echo endlessly here, the way her every whisper did. There was a flare of light, a glow that illuminated his face for a moment, making it come alive with light and shadow as if he were some sort of undulating demon. But then he leaned over, and in a moment the glow spread as he touched the match to the tapers in a silver candelabra, lighting them one by one. And lifting it, he moved around the room, lighting others. It seemed to Rachel there must be candles everywhere in this place. By the time he returned to her side, the entire room glowed with them, shadows leaping and dancing, soft yellow light spilling over everything.

He took her hand. Drew her forward. Rachel went with him, her fear dispelled as her curiosity leapt to the fore. The room was as big as a barn, and high, high above her, she saw something glittering in the candleglow. "Is that a chandelier?"

Donovan looked up, then nodded. "The entire place is equipped with gas lights, but I'll need to connect the main line and open the valves before they'll be of any use."

"What I wouldn't give to see this place in the daylight," she breathed. She felt him tense and wondered why.

Twin fireplaces stood at opposite walls, each one laid ready, waiting only to be lit. Each one had a huge stone mantel, and above them tapestries hung. Breathtaking tapestries. She moved closer to the one nearest her, covering Donovan's hand with her own to lift the candelabra higher. "They must be ancient," she muttered.

"Quite old, medieval, or so Dante said."

Her spine prickled. "Dante said that, did he?"

Donovan looked down at her rather quickly. "Or so the story goes. I'm only repeating what's been told to me."

She tilted her head, studying his face in the soft glow. "Are you, now?"

Nodding, he moved her to the left of the fireplace, lifting the light again and nodding toward the wall, where two crossed swords hung. "The broadswords are medieval as well, but Irish, whereas the tapestries are Italian."

"This Dante must have been quite a collector."

Donovan shrugged and moved on, pointing out other relics fastened to the walls, a suit of armor standing in a corner, looking ridiculously short, and the furnishings. Large chairs with embroidered cushions and elaborately carved, utterly straight backs, were grouped around the fireplaces. A large, ornate table with smaller, less elaborate chairs surrounding it held the room's center, each of its legs the size of a small tree. And there were weapons everywhere. Lances, maces, shields with their crests emblazoned across the front.

And every so often, they'd pass an archway of darkness, leading off into some other part of the castle. Each time, she'd peer into the blackness, eyes narrow, eager to see more.

But each time, she saw nothing.

When they'd walked round the entire room, he led her to one of the cushioned chairs, setting the candles on a marble stand at its side. Then he turned and knelt before the fire, and a second later it blazed to life, though she'd never seen him strike a match.

She let the warmth rinse through her, chasing the chill of autumn away. And Donovan settled himself in the chair beside her.

"I'd offer you something to drink, but—"

"I know," she said. "You've only just arrived. I can't very well be expectin' your cupboards to be fully stocked so soon." She smiled at him. "'Twill be cold...lonely, living here in this place, don't you think?"

He nodded. "Yes. But there's a history here I needed to…touch. I had to come back."

"Come back? You have been here before, then?"

He blinked slowly, averting his eyes. "Long ago."

"In your childhood?"

"Something like that."

She nodded, not pushing him further, though she was fully aware he hadn't really answered her. He couldn't have been the man who saved her from the river. That was twenty years ago. He was far too young. "Is this—this great hall—the only room you're willing to show me, then, Donovan?"

"For now," he told her. "It wouldn't be safe to take you farther…" A long pause as his gaze burned into hers. "Without more light."

Her throat went dry. She tried to swallow, and found she couldn't. He had a hungry look about him, a predatory look that shook her.

"Perhaps I should go then. Leave you to get settled in."

"Perhaps," he said.

Nodding, she got to her feet. He rose as well. "I…I'd like to come back. To talk to you about the legend."

"I don't know much about that. You'll be disappointed."

"I get the feelin' you know more about it than anyone else, Donovan O'Roark." She turned and walked toward the door, and he trailed her. She sensed he was eager for her to go.

But when he pushed the huge door open, a blinding flash of lightning cut a jagged path across the sky. The rain slashed in at them, and thunder rumbled in the distance.

Closed within the huge stone walls, they hadn't even been aware of the change in the weather, and there wasn't a window to be seen in this room, she realized for the first time.

He stood motionless. Said nothing. Well, then, there was no way around it. She lowered her head and took a step out…only to feel his hands closing on her shoulders, drawing her back inside. She nearly sighed in relief.

"You can't walk back to the village in this." He said it as if he regretted it right to his bones.

"I could. I'm not sugar, Donovan, and I won't melt in a wee bit of rain."

He closed the door, lifted a hand and swiped the droplets from her face, and then her hair. "Not melt, but get soaked through and take sick, at the very least. Or worse, get crushed beneath a falling tree, or struck down in your tracks by a bolt of lightning. No, I can't let you leave."

"You sound sorry about that."

He nodded, surprising her by not denying it. "I like my privacy, Rachel. You'll do well to remember that about me."

"Oh."

He frowned at her. "What?"

Shrugging, she lifted her brows. "I guess I was thinkin' there might be some other reason my bein' here disturbed you so much. No matter though."

She was only half teasing him, and she thought he knew it. She was drawn to the man, in a way she didn't understand. It was as if some sort of spell were being worked on her, to make her….

She closed her eyes, gave her head a shake. "I believe I must be more sleepy than I realized."

"There should be some bedrooms made up," he said, his voice gentle. Did she detect a slight tremor in it?

"Lead the way, then."

He nodded, picking up the dancing candles once more "Best stay close to me, Rachel. I've no idea how safe the entire castle is, since only parts of it have been kept up. Besides, you could get lost very easily in these halls."

She nodded her assent, and as he led the way into the dark, vaulted corridors, she held tighter and tighter to his arm, aware that with every step she took she was leaving safety farther behind. Not that she feared him.

Oh, but she did.

The halls twisted, turned, veered off in countless directions. He took her up spiraling stairways that felt like tunnels, they were so narrow and dark. And then down more hallways.

"Donovan?"

He paused, and turned to look at her there in the darkness.

"Are you deliberately leading me round and round, only to keep me from knowing my way out?"

Solemnly, he shook his head. "Just the opposite, Rachel. The room is near a back exit. So you can leave first thing in the morning."

"And why would I wish to do that, when you could just as easily lead me out of here yourself?"

"I...I won't be here. I have a pressing engagement, I'm afraid. Very early. So by the time you wake up, I'll be gone."

Tipping her head back, she studied him. "Will you, now?"

"Yes. And Rachel, I want your promise that you'll do as I ask. Leave here in the morning. No snooping, or exploring. I've already told you, it could be dangerous."

Studying him a long moment, she said, "Is there something here you don't want me to see?"

He shook his head. "You have as big an imagination as those locals at the pub, don't you?"

She smiled. "Bigger. You wouldn't doubt it if you knew what I was thinkin' just now."

"And what was that?"

She lifted her brows and shoulders as one. "That perhaps

the reason you won't be here in the morning is because you have an adverse reaction to daylight. And that perhaps the reason you don't want me snooping about, is so I won't stumble upon the coffin where you rest.'' She threw her head back and laughed at her own foolishness, and the sounds of it echoed endlessly, long after she stopped. "I guess I still have a bit of that gullible child in me after all. Or maybe 'tis simply livin' in Dunkinny that's made me so imaginative.''

But he only stared at her until her smile died.

She bit her lip, and her hand trembled slightly as she lifted it to touch his face. "I've hurt your feelin's now, have I? I don't really think you're a vampire, Donovan. But just a man. A…a beautiful man.'' She lowered her gaze, not quite believing she was about to say what she was. "I hope you don't think it bold of me to tell you this. But I— I'd like to see you again. Not because of the legend, but just…just because.'' And still he said nothing. Lowering her hand, she rolled her eyes ceilingward and drew a short, sharp breath. "Landsakes, Donovan, say something, will you? Am I makin' a total fool of myself, or…''

"No.'' He reached out to brush a curl off her forehead. "In fact, I've been trying very hard not to…feel anything toward you, all evening.''

She felt the blood rush to her face. "Oh.'' Then, licking her lips, meeting his eyes again, she whispered, "Why were you trying so hard not to feel that way, Donovan?''

"Because nothing can come of it.''

Her heart squeezed. "You're married, then.''

"No. Of course not. It's just…'' He shook his head. "You'll have to trust me, Rachel. Nothing can come of this. I…I probably won't even be here very long, and besides that, I—''He sighed deeply. "It doesn't matter. Here, this is your room.''

He pushed a door open and stepped inside.

Rachel followed, drawing a deep breath as the candle-light spilled on a canopied bed draped in sheer fabric of softest ivory. "'Tis beautiful."

"It's been restored. This is the room Dante had made ready for Laura Sullivan, the woman who betrayed him."

"My…my heartless ancestor slept here?"

"No. No, she killed him before she ever saw it."

Rachel turned toward him, a new idea creeping into her mind. "Are you puttin' me here, Donovan, so you won't forget whose blood runs in my veins?"

He didn't answer, only lowered his head.

"But you can't possibly blame me for what my forebears did."

"No. And I don't. I simply thought…" He shook his head. "I honestly don't know what I thought."

She took a step closer, drawn to him beyond reason, and driven by more than her usual boldness. She felt as if she knew him, as if she'd always known him, and there was no hint of shyness, and no earthly reason to temper her actions. Simply being near him seemed to have stripped her inhibitions away. "I can tell you what I think, Donovan O'Roark," she said. And when he looked up, she moved still closer. "I think you haven't the nerve in you to kiss me good-night."

His lips quirked, as if he wanted to smile and was fighting it. "Do you? Is that meant as a challenge, Rachel Sullivan?"

"Indeed, it is. I don't like this idea of you fightin' so hard to dislike me. An' I know that if you kiss me once, you'll forget about all that nonsense my ancestors did to yours, and simply see me. Not Alicia, nor Laura, but me. Rachel Sullivan."

He started to shake his head.

"I dare you," she whispered. "But I don't think you've the nerve."

His eyes darkened and she knew she'd won. He set the candelabra down on a nightstand and he came toward her, a distinct purpose glowing in his midnight eyes.

Chapter 5

I moved closer to her, compelled by some force I couldn't begin to understand. But my lips merely brushed across hers, their touch light, fleeting. For her mouth was not my goal. Not yet. Part of me wished to frighten her, I think, but there was more. To taste her...I longed for it with a hunger more powerful than the preternatural bloodlust I'd lived with for so long. And for a moment—only a moment—perhaps I forgot where I was. Perhaps part of my mind slipped backward to the time when Dante and I lived like kings, feared by the villagers. The times when we dared walk among them at night, before they understood what we truly were. Those times when, should a maid strike our fancy, we were free to take her, to drink our fill from her pretty throat, and use the power of our vampiric minds to make her remember it only as a dream. Those times before we were fully aware just how dangerous it was to interact with mortals in any way.

I reverted, I think, in my mind that night. So my lips

brushed across hers, and then across her cheek, and over her delicate jaw, and she knew. She knew on some level. Her head tipped back, to give me access to what I wanted. Her chin ceilingward as the breath shivered out of her. My lips found the skin of her neck; the spot where a river of blood rushed just beneath the surface. Its current thrummed louder, overwhelming my senses. Her scent, her texture…my head whirled. And my lips parted, and I tasted her then. The salt of her skin, warm on my tongue. Her pulse, throbbing faster against my lips. I drew the skin into my mouth, just a little, suckling her, allowing my teeth to press down ever so slightly.

Shuddering, she pushed herself closer to me, her body tight to mine—from the spot where my mouth teased her throat, to her breasts, straining against my chest, to her hips, arching forward, rubbing softly against mine and making me hard with wanting her.

My arms were around her, one hand cradling her upturned head, one cupping a softly rounded buttock and pulling her harder against me. Hers were on my head, fingers twisting and tugging at my hair as I sucked at her throat. I wanted to pierce her flesh. She wanted it too, I sensed that in everything she did, every soft sigh that whispered from her lips. But she didn't know what it was she was craving. She would though. She would.

I bit down harder, my incisors pinching, pushing against the soft flesh, preparing to break through that luscious surface to the nectar it concealed.

She gasped. A harsh, startled sound louder than the blast of a cannon to my ears, so focused was I on the taste of her. But it was enough to bring me back to myself, to make me realize what I'd been about to do.

The desire burned through me like a flame, and I trembled all over, a quake that utterly racked me as I forced myself to step away from her—to raise my head from her throat, and lower my arms to my sides and step away.

She didn't react immediately. And I knew too well why; could see it in the wide and slightly dazed look in her eyes. The allure of the vampire—and something more, too. Perhaps she'd felt the impact of this force between us as powerfully as I. Even I didn't understand it fully. To her, it would be even less comprehensible.

She came back to herself within a moment, blinking as if to clear her vision, and then staring up at me. "I don't think I've ever been…kissed…quite that way before." Lifting a hand, unaware she did so, she ran her fingertips slowly over the spot where my mouth had been.

"I…shouldn't have done that."

"Why did you?" she asked me.

I shook my head. "I'm not sure, Rachel. Perhaps for the same reason you allowed it."

Tilting her head to one side to study me, she frowned. Her hair slid away, revealing her neck to me again, and I felt a rush of renewed desire as I saw the redness forming there, and the moisture, and the way her fingers kept touching the spot and drawing away.

"Go to sleep," I whispered, but it was more than a whisper. I flexed the astral muscle, the one that didn't exist physically but was there all the same, the one that sent my wishes out to the minds of others. "Forget this happened." I caught her eyes with mine, sending the force out to her, the command that must be obeyed. "Forget the kiss, Rachel. It never happened. Go to sleep, and when you wake—"

"Oh, I doubt I'll sleep at all, Donovan O'Roark," she whispered with a soft, shaky smile. A bit of the mischief returned to her pretty eyes. "But forgettin' that kiss is certainly not an option whether I do or not. I'll either lie awake thinkin' about it, or go to sleep and dream it up again."

Her smile broadened. "'Twas a rather nice kiss, you know."

I stepped backward, an instinctive act, rather like reeling in shock, I thought later. She didn't react to the mind control at all. It hadn't...it hadn't even given her pause.

I realized I was standing in the hall now, when she reached for the candelabra and offered it to me. "You should take this with you, to find your way."

"No," I blurted, still trying to puzzle out her lack of a reaction to my commands, too much so to censor myself, fool that I was. "I see perfectly well in the dark." I could have kicked myself the moment the words left my lips.

"Can you, now?" She drew the glowing tapers back to her side. "I'll leave you to it, then. Good night, Donovan."

And she closed the door.

I stood there, trembling. Never had I been so drawn to a mortal before. And never, not ever in two hundred years, had I been so ineffective in influencing the thoughts of one of them. Making them forget. This told me two things. That her will was very strong, and that she didn't *want* to forget.

And she was here, in my home, my haven. God, what if she learned more than she should? What then?

Rachel closed the door, leaned against it, lowered her head and closed her eyes. She was shaking so hard she could barely stand, and she'd been terrified he'd see it before he left. She'd hidden it, she thought. Pulled the mask into place in time. Assumed the demeanor of the flirtatious, irreverent, and slightly cocky barmaid to conceal the depth of her reactions to him.

My God. The way he'd kissed her...the way his mouth had, not just caressed, but devoured her...and then the feel of those...

Those teeth!

She stood bolt upright, still shaking, but no longer weak.

Her hands flew to her neck once more, fingers searching, feeling, terror creeping over her soul. Had he…?

Diving into her deep pockets, she extracted a compact, struggled to open it, dropped it, and scrambled to snatch it up again. Finally, she leaned over the glowing candle flames, staring into the small, round mirror at the red mark on her neck. But there were no telltale puncture wounds, and there was no blood.

Just a small patch of bruised skin.

What her friends in the States called a hickey.

"Lord a' mercy," she breathed, snapping the compact shut, sagging once more. "I don't know whether to be weak with relief or to question my sanity for thinking…" Shaking her head, she drew herself upright, turned and went to the bed, taking the candles with her. She set them on a nightstand, and well away from the bed curtains that draped down from the canopy to swathe the thing in luxury. Beyond the sheer fabric, a red satin comforter swelled from the stacks of pillows beneath it, and when she pulled it back it was to find sheets of the same fabric, only black, not red.

The pulse in her throat beat a little harder.

She had no nightclothes here. But the bed hardly seemed made for such things.

Glancing quickly back toward the door, she saw the lock there, waiting to be turned. She saw it, licked her lips, and turned toward the bed once more. This time, to begin undressing.

And she slid naked into that decadent satin nest, felt its cool softness caressing her heated flesh, surrounding her in sensual pleasure. Cushioned and covered and enveloped within it. And when she fell asleep it was to dream of things more carnal than she'd ever done before.

She woke to the morning sunlight streaming through the window and bathing her face—and she was more curious about the man than ever before.

She flung the covers aside, got to her feet, naked in the chilly bedroom. Her clothes lay folded on a chair, just as she'd left them. She glanced at the unlocked door. He'd said he would be gone by the time she woke. But it was still early. Maybe…

She dressed quickly. Over and over his voice rang in her head. *Don't snoop. Leave by the back door as soon as you wake. I value my privacy.*

It would be wrong to go against his wishes, after he'd been so kind to her, letting her in when he obviously didn't want to. Letting her stay when he'd seemed almost afraid to.

Why?

She finished dressing, ran her fingers through her hair in lieu of a comb, and checked her appearance in the compact mirror since there were none to be found in the bedroom itself.

No mirrors?

She shook the thought away and examined her reflection. She looked storm-tossed. Wild. Hardly studious, much less virginal, and probably more like a barmaid than she ever had.

Why?

Him. His kiss, and a night spent reliving it beneath the caress of satin sheets that reminded her of his eyes.

"Damn," she whispered, and quickly made the bed before heading out the door, into the hall. Light now. Dim, for lack of windows, but enough light made its way in to see by. The door that led out of here was obvious. At the end of the hall to her right stood a tall, wooden door, with light glowing from beyond its thick pane of glass. Swallowing hard, stiffening her spine, mustering her willpower, she marched toward it, found it unlocked, and pulled it open.

Warm Irish sun bathed her face, her eyes. Stretching before her, like the crooked, graying teeth of a very old crocodile, were the crumbling stone steps, curving intimately down this tower's outer wall and disappearing round its other side. From here she could see the sea, glittering blue-green, with white froth roiling as the waves crashed against the rocky shore. The cliffs were almost directly below her.

The steps were probably perfectly safe.

"But he kept goin' on about the place perhaps bein' dangerous," she muttered to herself. "No, I really do believe he'd want me to go out the front way. Indeed, if he were here, he'd likely insist."

She stepped back inside and closed the door. Then she put her back to it, and faced a long, twisting corridor lined with doors, and open archways leading into other halls, or stairways going up or twisting downward. Shrugging her shoulders and battling an excited smile, she whispered, "I suppose I'll just have to search until I find a safer way out, won't I?"

Chapter 6

She got lost. Hopelessly, frighteningly lost. Lord, but she'd never realized how large this castle was, or how its corridors writhed about upon themselves like serpents in ecstasy. And so few windows! She no longer had any sense, even of what floor she might be wandering. Her only means of navigation was to try to go toward lighter areas, and away from the darker ones. But even this plan had its flaws, for she could only go so far before the light began to fade. Her choice then became, walk into the darkness or go back to where she'd already been. And going back would serve no purpose.

She made many discoveries that day. Some pleasant ones, but mostly unpleasant in the extreme. She discovered how thirsty she could become in a single day. How gruesome it was to walk face first into a sticky spider's web in the dark. How much she valued a good breakfast when one was unavailable.

Some of the more pleasant discoveries diverted her from

her misery for short spans of time. She spent hours exploring rooms full of fascinating antiques, and when she was tired, took a nap on a satin chaise fit for a queen. Later, she stumbled upon the music room, where a harpsichord rested, dusty and old. The soft cushioned window seats built into the stone wall. She sat on one to rest, and caught her breath as she gazed out over what surely must be all of Ireland. She was up so high. She'd been up and down so many stairways that she'd lost track, and truly had no clue where she'd ended. Now she knew, though the knowledge did her little good, except to tell her she ought to be going down. And down some more. And doing it soon, for from this vantage point she could see that the sun now rested on the very edge of the horizon, and would soon sink out of sight. She must have napped longer than she realized.

She lingered there only a short time. She might have stayed longer, despite the late hour, but she made the mistake of leaning over the old instrument, her fingers just lightly caressing the keys. And it let out a belch of sound that nearly stopped her heart. After that she had to be out of the room. Ridiculous, the feeling that pervaded her senses then, but no use denying it. She had the distinct sense that she must get out before Donovan learned she was here. And that blast from the harpsichord might have given her away, even told him exactly where she was, had he heard it.

She ran from the room, back into the snakepit of corridors, and took the first set of stairs she found that led downward.

Only they led into darkness. Or perhaps it was that night was falling now. She kept going down, and the stairs twisted, circling and spiraling, lower and lower. She kept one hand pressed to the walls on either side to keep from falling as she continued endlessly downward. And yet there seemed no end. She began to feel stifled, constricted by the walls at her sides, and even imagined them narrowing. Tightening. Squeezing in on her as if she'd been dropped into a funnel.

The stone step beneath her foot crumbled, and she drew back quickly, listening as the bits of it clattered and echoed into the darkness. She could no longer see at all. And that might have meant full night had fallen, or perhaps it was only that no light could penetrate this narrow spiraling staircase, all encased in stone.

"Enough," she muttered. "I'm goin' back."

And she turned, but her foot slipped, as a still larger chunk of the stone step fell away. It bounded down, crashing like the feet of a giant. And then there was another sound. Soft at first, light. Like the gentle beat of wings and a timid cry...

And then louder.

Screaming.

The air above her filled with rapidly beating wings and piercing shrieks as the bats that falling stone had startled awake swarmed above and around her. Blind beasts! Her scream joined their unearthly voices as she flailed her arms, but they battered her, colliding with her one after another, only to bound off in another direction. She felt them hitting her. Their small, furry bodies wriggling, and those rubbery wings pumping madly. Tiny clawed feet, scraping her face and moving on. Wetness—God alone knew what that was.

She screamed and beat at them, turning in circles and covering her face with her arms.

And then she tumbled.

Head over heels, her body hurtled down the staircase, bounding up and crashing down onto the uneven stone again and again. Smashing against the curving wall, only to rebound from it and follow the downward spiral. No bats now. She'd fallen past them and their mad flight. And for a single moment she thought the fall would be endless.

She came to a stop some seconds before she realized it. Her head still spun and her body screamed in pain from a hundred bruises, each one throbbing as if it were being beaten anew. But gradually, the sense of motion faded, and she realized she was still. She lay on her side, more or less, though her limbs were twisted and bent in unnatural angles.

Slowly, she pulled herself upright, into a sitting position. Every movement hurt. Every spot on her body cried out in protest at her cruelty in moving it at all. But gradually, she did, getting her arms and legs into a more natural state, checking them to be sure they still functioned properly. Nothing seemed to be broken. At least, she could move everything.

God, but it hurt!

Slowly, inch by inch, her hands on the wall nearest her, she pulled herself to her feet. Her trouble, she realized, had not ended simply because her fall had. She still needed to find her way out of this castle. For the first time it occurred to her that she might be trapped here indefinitely. She could starve, or die of thirst before anyone found her.

And somehow the thought didn't frighten her as much as the thought of being found...

But that was foolish.

The stairs had ended, and she was now on a level floor, more or less, though there were chips and breaks in the stone that made walking precarious at best. Still, she made her way forward, wishing for nothing so much as a candle to see by...

The lighter.

She quickly dipped into her pocket and praised her lucky stars, it was still there. She lit it, held it out in front of her, and saw that she was in a long, wide corridor of stone and utter darkness—very much like a cave. But in the distance, doors stood, silent and closed. Perhaps one would lead to…to somewhere.

Her footsteps echoed—unevenly, since she was limping now—as she made her way down the hall, and paused before the first doorway. Pushing it open, she found only an empty room. So she moved on to the second. And of course, an empty room greeted her there, as well.

Only one door remained. Her heart in her throat, tears of frustration beginning to burn in her eyes, she touched the handle.

Locked.

A sob welled up to choke off her breath, and she lowered her head to the wood to cry.

But then there was a sound. A soft creaking sound…a sound that came from beyond that door.

Like another door of some kind, opening….slowly opening.

Straining to hear, she pressed closer, listening with everything in her. Gentle taps upon the floor. Someone moving around. Then a flare of light from beneath, one that grew brighter.

The steps came closer. And something…something made her back away.

The door opened with a deep, forbidding moan of protest.

She looked into the eyes of Donovan O'Roark, saw them widen with shock and something that might have been fear—perhaps even panic. And then she managed to tear her gaze from his to look past him into the room, where candles glowed now. There was nothing there…nothing except a large, gleaming coffin, its lid standing open, its satin lining aglow in the candlelight.

Black and red, the satin inside that box. Black and red like the satin in which she'd slept.

She backed away.

He reached for her.

She whirled, the lighter falling from her hands, and then she ran.

"Rachel! Rachel, wait!"

Panic bubbled in her chest, larger and larger, expanding until she felt the bubble would burst and she'd die, right there, from the force of the fear that possessed her. She fled, headlong, having no idea where she was going, what she would do.

But she knew he pursued her. She knew he'd catch her soon, and Lord help her, what would she do then? What?

The hallway ended. Abruptly, and without a hint of warning in the pitch blackness. She heard Donovan's voice shout a warning—one she ignored—and then she felt the solid, skin-razing wall of stone stopping her heedless flight with a single blow. Her head, her body, the impact rocked her to the teeth and to the bone. But the head was the worst, and she felt the warmth of blood running from the wound and stinging her eyes as she sank slowly to the floor.

"My God, Rachel…"

He was upon her like a wolf on an injured lamb, and she knew she no longer had a chance. She'd die here in this dungeon or whatever it was. She'd die here, bloodless and pale, and the vampire would have his vengeance on the females of the Sullivan clan at last.

He knelt beside her, gathering her into his arms and leaning over her. She felt his breath on her face. His fingers, probing the pulsing wound on her forehead. "Damn fool woman, you could have got yourself killed!"

As if he wasn't planning to finish that job himself, she thought, groggy now, fading fast.

He got to his feet and carried her back down the hall, through one of the other doors, where she'd seen nothing, and right up to the wall. She tried weakly to leap from his embrace, which likely would have resulted in cracking her head again, this time on the floor, but his arms tightened around her. "Be still, Rachel."

"Let me go…let me go…" She twisted, pulled against him, but his arms were like steel. He paused there beside the wall, lifted one hand, holding her captive quite easily with the other. He touched something and the wall moved, backing away and leaving a two-foot gap on either side. Donovan carried her through that gap, and she caught her breath as the wall closed off again. He moved left, up a single flight of stairs, these ones broad and solid, rather than narrow and crumbling like the ones where she'd fallen. Then he touched another wall, this one at the top of the staircase, and it opened like a door.

He stepped out, and lowered her down onto a soft settee, and then he turned to a wall, and did something. Moments later a soft light suffused the room from above, growing brighter until the place was perfectly well lit.

The light above her was, she realized, the gas-powered chandelier. And the room around her was the great hall.

"So close…I was…so very close…"

"To what, Rachel? To escape?"

She closed her eyes, touched her throbbing head. He ignored her for the moment, intent on lighting first one fire and then the other as she lay there. She felt the heat, saw the light.

"If it was escape you wanted, why didn't you leave by the back door when you awoke this morning? Why did you insist on doing the one thing I asked you not to do?"

He turned to face her, she saw as she peered at him, but the sight of the flames in the fireplace, reflected in his dark hair and deep blue eyes, only made her head hurt more, so she quickly closed her eyes once again. "I wasn't snooping. I…the back stairs looked unsafe. I was only tryin' to find a saner way to leave this ruin."

He was closer now. Right beside her. "You're lying," he whispered.

"No—"

He gripped her shoulders, lifting her slightly, and readying, she thought, to do her in. But his hands closed on bruised flesh, and she winced in agony.

Donovan went utterly still. Then, frowning, he pushed her hair aside, eyeing her face, her neck. "My God, you're more injured than I realized."

That he was choosing to ignore the fact that she'd all but seen him rise from a coffin would have been amusing, if she hadn't been so certain her death was imminent. "I fell," she told him. "Down a long flight of stairs…the bats frightened me, and I lost my footing…" She bit her lip as the memory of it came up to choke off her words.

Sighing deeply, he gripped her shirt at its hem, and without even asking her consent, he tugged it over her head. Then he touched her, with his eyes as well as his hands, examining the bruises and scrapes she'd suffered.

"I'm all right," she told him. "Nothing's broken."

He nodded as if in agreement, but took a handkerchief, spotlessly white, from a pocket and pressed it to her wounded head. "I'll find some ice for this."

"I don't want ice. I just want to leave. Please…"

He shook his head slowly. "Why? I thought you wanted to know all my secrets."

She clamped her mouth closed, swallowing hard. His gaze moved, heating as it did, over her body. She felt naked, wearing no more than a bra and skirt. And the look in his eyes made her feel even more vulnerable and exposed.

"I've changed my mind. I'll find some other subject to write about. I just…just want to leave this place."

"And me, isn't that right, Rachel? Because you've discovered the monster of your nightmares. The demon of your childhood. The legend you refused to believe. All true, all real. All alive…in me.''

She met his eyes. "It's true, isn't it?"

"What do you think?"

She only shook her head. "I never believed you were evil. Tell me I wasn't wrong."

He said nothing, just stared at her.

"Don't kill me," she whispered. "I swear, I'll never tell a soul."

His smile was slow, and almost sad. "I'm not going to kill you, Rachel. And I already know you won't tell my secret."

She blinked, hope washing over her like a flood of warmth and sunlight. "You can trust me. I swear it, Donovan—"

"No," he said. "I can't trust you. That's why you're going to have to stay here."

Her brows rose high, eyes widening. "Stay here? But…but…" She didn't understand, couldn't comprehend. "For how long?"

He said nothing, but she could see his meaning in his eyes, could hear his deep voice tingle up her spine even though he never spoke the word. She heard it, in her soul.

Forever.

Chapter 7

She was as bruised and battered as if I'd beaten her. I felt her pain, in spite of myself, as I bathed each spot in cool water.

But she drew away, her eyes partly angry, but mostly afraid.

"Don't touch me. I won't stay, do you hear me? You have to let me go."

With my simple glance, an icy one, she stilled. And I resumed pressing the cool cloth to the bruises. "You will stay," I said.

"They'll worry about me in the village. They'll come looking."

Her breasts strained against the bra she wore. A small purple welt formed on one of them, and I pressed the cloth gently over it, not taking my hand away, but keeping it there. Feeling her warmth seeping into my palm. And the heat of desire flaring up from within.

She went utterly still, staring at my hand where it rested upon her breast. Her breaths coming shallow and quick.

"Be honest, Rachel. You didn't tell a soul where you were going."

She blinked, and I knew I was right.

"You'll send a note…to Mary at the pub, telling her you've gone traveling and don't know when you'll return."

"I'll do no such thing." And she pulled free of me, leaping to her feet, snatching her blouse from the settee and struggling into it.

"You will do exactly as I tell you, Rachel."

"Never." She surged toward the door, and I stood still, letting her make her foolish attempt. When she tugged, she found the entryway sealed tight. Locked. She went still, her back to me, hand still on the door, and her head slowly lowered. Softly, she whispered, "What are you, Donovan O'Roark? And what are you goin' to do with me?"

"I think you know what I am."

She turned very slowly, and I felt her gaze burning into me, searching my soul. "No. 'Tisn't possible. 'Tis…'tis some elaborate hoax."

"It's not only possible, but true. And I think you know it."

Her eyes narrowed, a little of the fear leaving them. She came nearer, studying me so closely I felt exposed to my bones. But she stopped before she reached me. "There are no such things as vampires," she whispered. "And the tale of Donovan O'Roark is but a legend. Not real."

I stood very still, wondering why I felt so vulnerable, why I was waiting in secret dread of her reaction when she finally realized the truth.

"That's it, isn't it? This is your idea of a joke. You're but tryin' to teach me a lesson." One step, then another, and she stood very close. "You're only trying to scare me, and for a time, you succeeded. But I've come to my senses now, Donovan. So why don't you simply tell me the truth rather than playing out this game and pretending you won't let me leave?''

Raising my hands, I let them rest gently on her shoulders. ''It is no game, Rachel. Tell me, why should I let you go the way Dante let Laura Sullivan go a century past? So you can run screaming through the village the way she did? So you can lead a mob back here at the break of dawn to end my miserable life?'' Closing my eyes very slowly, I whispered, ''Perhaps if I were wise I'd do just that.''

But I instantly regretted that impulsive declaration. When I opened my eyes again I saw her frowning at me. ''I won't believe any of it. If you're a vampire, prove it to me.''

Lowering my head, I shook it slowly. ''You have the talk of the villagers. The way they look at me when I pass…as if the devil himself is in their midst. What more proof do you need, lass?''

She shrugged her shoulders. ''Turn into a bat,'' she suggested.

I looked up quickly, sensing the edgy humor creeping into her voice. God, did she really believe this was all a joke? ''I'm afraid that's not a skill I've mastered. I've heard that shape-shifting is possible to the truly ancient ones among us. But I'm only two centuries old.''

''Barely old enough to drive,'' she mocked.

Closing my eyes, sighing deeply, I muttered, ''Do you have a mirror, Rachel?''

''A mirror?''

I nodded, not looking at her. She hesitated. Then, ''Look, d-don't you think you've carried this joke far enough? You knew I wouldn't leave as you told me, so you pulled that prank with the coffin, and your timing was perfect. Though how you could be sure I'd find you in this maze of crumbling stone—I mean, I could've been killed and it really wasn't all that amusing, and—''

''Get the mirror.'' I met her eyes, stared into them.

"Get the mirror, Rachel, and let's get this part of it over with, shall we?"

"You're a lunatic." She dug into her pocket. "This isn't going to prove a thing. I swear, you've made your point. I learned my lesson, my snooping days are over, and I..." She drew a compact out of her pocket, fingered it slowly, and I knew her fear was coming back. She fought it, but it was returning in spite of her skepticism.

"Open it," I told her. "And then you can go back to hating me the way the rest of them do."

"Don't be silly," she said. "They don't even know you." She opened the compact.

"They've known me for two centuries," I said. "I was one of them once." I took the mirror from her hands, bit my lip slightly. "Look, Rachel. See me for the monster everyone else does." And I held the mirror before my face.

She drew a deep breath, and moved around beside me. And then she gasped, and backed away. "It can't be...it can't be true."

I only stood where I was, snapping the despicable mirror closed and tossing it to the settee.

"Oh, it's true."

"And the legend? The tale of how you sat up in your own coffin and the priest tried..."

"Tried to kill me. My own father handed him the mallet and stake. My own mother called me a demon. And the girl I'd planned to marry screamed for my blood."

I heard her try to swallow, and the way she struggled to breathe. "And the rest of it? The belief that you'd return one day to destroy the village and take revenge on the Sullivan women?"

I lowered my head. "Do you believe that's why I've come home, Rachel?"

She blinked, and looked up into my eyes. "You said I couldn't leave. What do you intend to do with me?"

"I don't know."

"Am I in danger here?"

"If I said no, would you believe me?"

Her throat convulsed. "Let me leave, Donovan."

"You weren't so eager to leave me last night, Rachel. Or have you forgotten that kiss in your chamber?"

"That was before…"

"Before what? Before you knew the truth? That I'm a monster, bent on destruction and revenge? You know nothing about me, and yet you readily believe the worst."

For a moment she was silent. Then sighing, she said, "You're right. I'm behaving just the way the others do. Judging you, when I swore I never would. Exactly the way you believe the worst about me." And her words rocked me. "That I'd betray you simply because my ancestors did. That if you let me go, I'd shout your secrets to the world."

I lowered my head. She was right, that was exactly what I thought. "So we're at an impasse."

She huffed. Folded her arms across her chest. "Are you going to kill me?"

"No." Then I met her eyes. "Do you believe that?"

"I shouldn't, but for some reason I do."

"Good." I literally sighed in relief.

"Don't celebrate, Donovan. Part of the reason I believe it is because I want to. I'm only too aware that I'm likely kidding myself."

"I won't hurt you, Rachel, you have my word on that."

"Will you let me go?"

"I can't. Not…yet."

"When?"

"I don't know." I pressed both hands to my head and turned in a slow circle. "I have to think."

She stood still for a long moment. Then she blinked and looked at the ceiling. "I'm having some trouble believing all this. I should be screaming or running for my life, or fainting, shouldn't I?''

"You already did those things."

Her mouth quirked very slightly, a tremulous hint of a smile. "So how do most women react when you tell them you're a vampire?"

"I've never told another woman."

I didn't look at her when I said it. Instead I turned and walked toward the blazing fireplace, then lowered myself into a chair close to it, seeking the warmth. "But if I had, I imagine they'd have reacted the same way you did. First with horror, then disbelief, and now..." I turned to look back at her, where she still stood. "What are you feeling now, Rachel?"

She moved closer, taking the opposite chair. "I'm mad as hell at you, for keeping me here against my will. As for the other..." Shaking her head quickly side to side, she shrugged. "I'm not sure I know what to make of it. And there's one other thing I'm feeling, Donovan O'Roark."

A hint of panic tickled at my nape. "What?"

"Hunger."

She watched him, still battling an eerie sense of having fallen into some dream world. Dizzy with the weight of his revelations, not sure she believed what her own eyes had shown her, she was dazzled. But not terrified—or not as much as she had been at first.

He went away, leaving her to explore on her own, and she did, thumbing through the books in his bookcase, taking a closer look at the tapestries on his wall. She recalled last night. The kiss. The way his lips had trailed over her throat, and he'd tasted her skin there. The incredible sensations the touch of his mouth had evoked in her. Sensations she'd never felt before. Just at a kiss.

What had he been thinking? Was it the way it was depicted in fiction? Had he been battling some kind of mad bloodlust? Barely restraining himself from taking her life? And why wasn't she paralyzed with fear?

But she wasn't. She was curious now that the fear was beginning to ebb. And more. Still drawn to him as she'd always been. And only now beginning to realize that what she'd believed as a child…might very well be true. It was no longer impossible, was it?

She'd never feared the shadowy figure she saw as her protector when she'd been a child. And she wasn't afraid of him now. Nervous, uncertain, angry, curious. But not afraid.

She must be losing her grip on reality, for she certainly should be.

He appeared then, a bowl of soup steaming in his hands, a glass of something red beside it. As her gaze fell on the scarlet liquid and widened, she heard him mutter, "Wine," and immediately felt foolish.

Of course it was wine. What else would it be?

He set the soup on a marble stand, then moved it closer to her chair. She returned to her seat, eyeing the meal.

"It was the best I could do. The workers left a few supplies in the cupboards when they left this last time."

She tilted her head to one side. "And…what about you?"

He lowered his head. "Don't ask questions if you aren't prepared for the answers, Rachel."

"I don't think anyone can be prepared for something like this. Were you?"

His head came up quickly. "What do you mean?"

"Well…I mean, when you first…how did it happen to you?"

"Why do you want to know?"

She shrugged. "I…I just do. You're holding me prisoner here, the least you can do is make conversation."

"It isn't conversation, it's interrogation."

She scowled at him. "It's curiosity. Nothing more."

"It's a girl after a story. That paper, my secrets, as you said." He cleared his throat, staring at a spot just past her. "However, maybe it's for the best that you still want to know. I believe I've come up with a solution to our mutual problem here. A compromise."

"Oh?" She sipped soup from her spoon, and dipped in for more. It was hot, tasty. "A bargain, you mean?"

"Yes."

"Well, this is interesting. How can you make a bargain with me when you've already made it clear I'm stuck here whether I like it or not?"

"At least this way you'll get something in return."

"What?"

"Everything you want to know, Rachel. Stay with me, give me time to make certain…arrangements. Do this, and I'll tell you my story. And when I've done the things I need to do, I'll let you go."

She tilted her head to one side. "What kinds of arrangements are you speaking of, Donovan?"

I shrugged, unable to take my eyes from hers, openly curious, the fear fading bit by bit. "I'll need to change my name, establish a new identity, prepare a place for myself to live, a new place, where no one has seen me before."

Shaking her head slowly from side to side, she whispered, "But why?"

"Because you'll know all my secrets. And when you write your paper, others will know. They'll flock here in droves, some merely curious, others…others intent on my destruction."

"I think you're overreacting. No one would even believe it was true…"

"The locals already believe it."

She lowered her head. "This isn't 1898, Donovan. The angry mobs you envision are in your imagination."

"No," I said softly. "They're in my memory. I saw the best friend I'd ever had driven to his death, Rachel. I have no intention of ending my life that way. I won't."

She lifted her gaze to mine, probed my eyes. "I don't suppose I blame you." Then she set her bowl aside, still half filled, as if she'd lost her appetite. "You seem to have given this a lot of thought."

"I have."

"I believe there's one thing you haven't considered, Donovan." I looked at her, waited. She rose and paced to the hearth. Bracing her arms on the mantel she stared into the flames. Their light bathed her face, gleamed in her eyes. "You haven't credited me with an ounce of humanity. So it will come as a surprise to you to learn I am, indeed, human, since you seem to believe I'm the same sort of monster you keep calling yourself."

"I never implied—"

"I would never write a paper that would drive a man from his home, force him to give up his entire life. Why would I? For a degree? 'Tis hardly a fair exchange."

I searched her eyes, looking for the lie. But I didn't find it.

"None of this is necessary, Donovan. I'll simply find another subject for my paper."

My eyes narrowed. I almost wanted to believe her.

"Lord, but you think I'm lyin' to ya, don't you, Donovan?"

I had to look away. "You might be lying," I said. "Or you might be telling the truth. I can't be sure. And I'm afraid I can't risk taking you at your word."

"I've never broken my word in my life!"

She declared it with such fierceness it nearly shook my

resolve. Lowering my head, unable to face her, I whispered, "I'm sorry."

She faced me, then glanced beyond me toward the door, and when I managed to look at her again, there were tears building in her eyes. "You really are going to keep me here—like a prisoner—aren't you?"

"I have no choice, Rachel."

"The hell you don't, Donovan O'Roark. The hell you don't. You've been right about one thing, I'll grant you that. You truly *are* a monster. And not because you're a vampire, but because you have no heart. No trust. Nor a care for anyone besides yourself. Make your arrangements if you must. An' when you're ready to set me free, come fetch me."

Her anger washed over me like a tempest, and I actually staggered backward under its force. Then she whirled and stomped up the stairs, intent, I was certain, on finding her room, slamming its door and throwing the lock. And it would have been a very dramatic exit, too, if she hadn't paused, panting, halfway up the stone staircase. Without looking back she said, "Kindly guide me back to my room, O'Roark. I've no desire to become lost in this mausoleum again."

I nodded, and slowly mounted the stairs. When I got to her, I touched her elbow, cupped it in my hand, and she pulled away. "I am the way I am because I have to be," I said slowly as we moved up the stairs. "It's a matter of self-preservation. If Dante didn't teach me another thing, he taught me this. We're meant to be alone. To live alone. To trust no one. It's the only way we can survive. He forgot his own most important lessons. And he died because of it."

She'd stopped walking, and when I glanced down to see why, she was staring at me, still angry, but there was something else in her eyes as well. "Alone," she whispered.

"An' just how long have you been living by those words, Donovan?"

"Ever since Dante died," I told her softly.

"A hundred years..."

I shrugged and started walking again, touching her elbow, propelling her upward. "One gets used to it."

"No, I don't believe one does. 'Tis little wonder you've no idea how to behave toward another."

I turned at the head of the stairs, stopped before a large door. "I think you'll like this room better, Rachel. I...I had it decorated myself."

She blinked. "For whom?"

I looked at her. "I...for no one. It was a whim. A foolish whim." I pushed the door open, turned a knob affixed to the wall, and watched as the gaslights slowly came up. I'd connected the lines while she slept, ignited all the pilots, even cleaned the glass globes. I hadn't really expected her to leave as I'd ordered. But I hadn't expected her to find my resting place either.

She stepped past me into the room I'd had built for no imaginable reason. I remembered more than Dante's betrayal at the hands of a woman, and subsequent death. I also remembered my friend's happiness, the glow about him when he'd been in love, and believed himself loved in return. Even I had been hesitant to berate Dante or speak my doubts of Laura Sullivan's loyalty aloud. There must be no other happiness in the world like that of love.

And while I'd existed in utter solitude all this time, my mind had opportunity to wander. To wonder. To dream. What would it be like? What if it happened for me?

And that fantastical dream had inspired me to build these rooms. The suite I'd created for a dream lover I would never know. The rooms I would give to her if she were real. The rooms we would share.

Empty. They stood empty and likely always would.

Except for Rachel. For a few nights, they'd be filled with a woman whose beauty was worthy of them.

"Lordy, but this is lovely…" She stepped inside, twirling in a slow circle to take in the sheer mauve fabric draped from the bed's canopy to form curtains. The carpet, a similar color and so thick her feet left imprints as she moved. The glass doors, that opened out onto a stone balcony fit for a princess. The elaborately hand-tooled woodwork, painted gold to match the trim on the velvety wallpaper, and the tiebacks for the mauve drapes.

Her smile came, despite the situation. And I secretly relished it. The rooms were wasted with no one to enjoy them. That they gave her pleasure pleased some secret part of me.

"There's more," I told her, taking her hand and drawing her toward one of two doors. "The bath, here." She gasped at the sunken tub, the golden fixtures. Plump towels in deep green lined every rack, and deep rugs the same shade covered the floor. Bottles of expensive oils and fragrances lined the shelves.

"Who did you dream of entertaining here, Donovan? A queen?"

My lover. The one I would never know. But I didn't tell her that.

"There's a sitting room as well," I said, going back to the bedroom and pushing open a second door to reveal a room lined with bookshelves, two window seats, a small pedestal table with a pair of cushioned chairs, and a settee, sofa, and rocker. A fireplace laid ready, but unlit, and gas lamps lined the stone walls.

But she wasn't looking at the room. She was looking at me. "Why all this?" she whispered. "Why go to all this trouble if you truly intended to live your life alone, Donovan O'Roark?"

I shook my head. "As I said, a foolish whim."

"No, I don't think so." She came closer, tipping her

head back, searching my eyes. "You're lonely. And tired of being, I think."

"That has nothing to do with…" I lowered my eyes, my voice trailing off.

"With what? With why you're keeping me here?" She blinked and looked around her. "You might believe that, Donovan, but I don't think it's true. I think you built this room with every intention of bringing someone here to fill it. To fill…you."

I turned fully now, glancing at the fireplace as if it fascinated me and trying not to tremble in fear at her words. "Thinking that way will only confuse you, Rachel. I need no one. I share my life with *no one*. You're here because I cannot let you leave. But I will, the moment my arrangements are made and it's safe for me to do so. That's all. There is no more to it than that."

I felt her staring at my back. "All right. If you say so."

I turned to go. She stayed silent as I stepped into the hall and closed the door. And then I stood there, trembling.

God, could she be right?

Chapter 8

"All the modern conveniences," she muttered, alone in her suite of rooms. He'd gone, left her here on her own, and he probably believed she preferred it that way.

She didn't. This place was too large, too hollow and quiet. Like a tomb. She soaked in a tub brimming with steamy water, and sprinkled some of the aromatic oils in with her. Her bruises needed the pampering, and the heat did ease her aches somewhat.

But she'd have to put her torn, dirty clothes back on when she got out, and the idea didn't appeal. She didn't suppose he'd let her go long enough to rush back to her room above the pub and fetch her own things. So would he expect her to spend her entire time here in the same clothing?

Moreover, did he expect her to spend it alone, in these rooms?

He couldn't. She wouldn't stand for that.

When the water began to cool, she got out, wrapped

herself in a thick green towel, and stepped back into the bedroom. The double doors of a built-in wardrobe beckoned, and she went slowly toward them, hesitantly reached out, and pulled them open.

"Lordy..." The closet nearly spilled over with clothing. Satins, silks and lace in a hundred shades cascaded from hangers.

To one side were drawers built into the wall, and as she tugged them open she found nightgowns almost too fragile to touch, and underthings.

"But why?" She touched the garments, pulled the hangers along the rack one by one, saw that the sizes varied as widely as the colors and fabrics did. She paused at a long full skirt, paired on the hanger with a white off-the-shoulder blouse. It looked like something a Gypsy might wear.

"Take anything you like."

She caught her breath and whirled, automatically clutching at the towel around her. "Donovan. I didn't hear you come in."

"I expected the door to be locked."

She blinked, saying nothing. But as she searched his eyes this time, she saw the pain there. The loneliness. He'd built these rooms on a whim, he'd said. But it was obvious to her he'd prepared them for a woman. Was she real? she wondered. Or only some distant wish he'd allowed himself to indulge in secretly?

When she still didn't speak, he took a step backward, his hand still on the doorknob. "I'm sorry. I'll leave you alone."

"No, don't go."

He stopped abruptly, looking at her. And she saw his gaze dip beyond her face, very briefly touching on her body, covered only by a towel. And she knew her bruises showed, and her hair was damp and tangled, hanging over her shoulders. And still she felt some deep reaction to that gaze. As if it were truly admiration in his eyes, and not only surprise.

"You…want me to stay?"

She turned back to the closet, removing the clothes she'd been drawn to, not looking at him. "If you're going to keep me here, Donovan, the least you can do is entertain me. I'll go crazy if I'm to spend all my time in these rooms alone. Lovely though they are, I'd soon die of boredom."

He lowered his head. "I…thought you'd want to rest."

"It's too early to rest. Besides, if I'm to sleep all night and you're to sleep all day…" She blinked, and tilted her head to one side. "You do, don't you?"

He only nodded.

"Well, then how are you going to keep to our bargain? When will you have time to tell me all your secrets, Donovan?"

He brought his gaze level with hers quickly, and a frown marred his brow. "So you've decided to write the paper after all?"

She shrugged, draping the clothes over her arm and heading toward the bathroom. "You can believe what you wish. You will anyway. The truth is, I'm curious."

"That's all?" he asked.

She paused in the doorway to glance back at him. "Yes. That's all. I'll only be a minute." And she closed the door. Quickly, she donned the skirt, long and loose, and moving around her like a spring breeze. Then the blouse, its sleeves dipping low on her shoulders, and the elastic waistline clinging high enough so that a bit of her midriff was visible. She ran a brush through her hair, frowning at the lack of a mirror in the room.

No mirrors. As if, even in his fondest fantasies, he hadn't allowed himself to imagine a mortal woman filling his loneliness. Only another creature like him.

She didn't fit the bill in the least, did she?

She blinked, and then frowned hard. It didn't matter! What made her think such a thing? Oh, but she knew. Was knowing more and more with each moment that passed. He was that gentle soul who'd pulled her from the river, he was that dark angel who'd comforted her when she'd cried in her bed, alone and afraid. And she'd loved him all her life.

He didn't trust her. She wasn't even certain she could blame him for that. She was a Sullivan.

But she was meant to set it right, she sensed that. She was meant for him.

Finally, clearing her throat and gathering her wits about her, she stepped back into the bedroom.

Donovan looked her up and down, blinking as if in surprise.

"It's hardly modern," she said, fingering the fabric of the skirt.

"It's lovely. *You're* lovely."

She averted her face, feeling the heat creeping into her cheeks. "These rooms are so different from the rest of the castle…so is the great hall."

"Actually, it's only the north wing that's still in disrepair. Unfortunately, that's where you ended up earlier. Most of the place has been restored, updated." He reached out to move her hair off her forehead, and gingerly examined the bump there, a result of her collision with the wall. "There's even electricity."

"But you use the gas lamps?"

"I prefer them. Are you hurting much, Rachel?"

"I'm sore, but only a wee bit. I'll be fine," she told him. She eyed the soft golden glow emanating from the fixtures in the room and nodded. "I agree, the gas lamps are far nicer. Will you show me around, then? Um…the restored parts, I mean. I've no interest in seeing the north wing again."

"That's good. I'm afraid that wing is off-limits while you're here, Rachel."

She searched his face. "So there are some secrets you won't be sharing with me?"

His eyes hooded, he shook his head. "The north wing is unsafe, as you've already learned. Stay out of it, Rachel."

Her curiosity rose to new heights. "All right," she said. She didn't think he believed her.

"Come." He offered his arm.

She took it. Closed her hand around his upper arm, and felt him. Warm, not cold as one might expect. He felt real. He felt like a man. Not a monster.

He had, she mused, the deepest, bluest eyes she'd ever seen, and hair a soft, dark brown, nearly black. She'd been incredibly attracted to him at first. And she still was.

He led her through the main hall of this wing. Showing her other bedrooms, none in use, but many ready for company. Odd, for a man who expected to be alone forever. Then he guided her back down the stairs, where he showed her the library, a huge room lined with books on shelves that towered to the ceilings. Leather chairs sat in pairs by the towering windows.

"'Tis a sad room," she said, speaking in muted tones as if she were at a funeral.

"Sad? Why do you say so?"

She walked forward slowly, pausing between two chairs beside a tall window that was completely enshrouded by heavy velvet drapes. "The seats...they're in pairs. All of them. But you've no one to sit in them with you."

When she glanced back at him, he only shrugged. She turned forward again, and fingered the deep honey velvet. "It's as if the world is a place you'd rather not see. But it's too beautiful to shut out, you know."

Stepping forward, he pulled the cord and opened the drapes. "Yes, I know."

She glanced out, then drew a surprised breath. The windows looked out on a flagstone path that meandered amid lush shrubs and bushes she couldn't identify. In the center, the moonlight glistened on a fountain, ancient, but completely restored. A stone image of some pagan goddess stood on a pedestal, spilling clear water from her outspread palms to splash into the pool spreading below her.

"'Tis beautiful," she whispered, but then she drew her gaze away, staring in confusion at the other windows, their draperies drawn tight.

"They're only drawn by day, Rachel. As soon as darkness falls, I part them." He looked past her, into his garden. "I love the night."

"And the daylight?" she asked, in a voice that emerged as a bare whisper.

"It would kill me. The way it killed Dante." He turned to face her. "Would you like to walk in my garden?"

"Yes. Yes, I'd like that very much."

He reached for her hand. He seemed to make a habit of doing that. She let him take it, though, and followed as he led her to the far end of the library, to yet another set of drapes. These parted to reveal French doors, that opened onto the garden.

"It's larger than I could tell from the window."

Nodding, he cradled her hand in his, perhaps unaware of doing so. Or maybe not. "It stretches out on this side, and around to the rear of the castle, reaching nearly to the cliffs."

She fingered a delicate-looking vine that clung to the castle wall. Narrow green buds nodded heavily from it. "I've never seen this before."

"Wait," he told her. "We'll sit. Here." He pointed to a stone bench with claw feet and lion's heads for arms. They went to it, sat down.

"Is that why you rest by day? Because you can't be exposed to sunlight?"

He turned toward her. "Not entirely."

She only waited, willing him to answer while he searched her face for…something. Her true evil intent, she imagined.

"As daylight approaches our functions begin to slow. By dawn we're usually unconscious, whether we want to be or not. And it's not the sort of sleep from which one can be roused."

"Like…death?"

"Not so deep as death, I imagine. But far deeper than any mortal's sleep."

"So if someone were to poke you, or shake you or shout in your ear….."

"Or set me aflame or drive a stake through my heart," he finished for her. "I'd be aware of it, but likely unable to react enough to defend myself."

"That must be frightening."

"It's the reason for the coffins, hidden in the bowels of the castle. I'm most vulnerable while I rest…and why I'm telling you any of this I can't say."

"Maybe you're starting to trust me?"

"I trust no one, Rachel. Beautiful mortal females least of all."

She blinked. "You…find me beautiful?"

He stared at her for a long moment, and his eyes seemed to heat as they moved lower, raking her before slowly meeting hers again. Then he simply turned away, facing the castle, and the curious vines.

"Look."

She looked. Then she caught her breath as one by one, the green buds seemed to split. Bit by bit they opened, milk-white petals unfurling, their faces turning up to the moon as if in welcome. Welcoming the night.

"I've never seen anything like them."

"They're very rare. Moon lilies. I had them imported."

"They're beautiful." As she looked around, she noticed other plants in bloom.

"I have no flower that closes up by night. Everything either remains open through the dark hours, or only blooms in darkness."

"It makes sense. Day lilies or morning glories would be wasted here."

He nodded.

Rachel yawned, quickly covering her mouth with her hand.

"It's late," he said. "You've had an exhausting day. You should rest now."

She tilted her head to one side. "I can always sleep late in the morning. 'Tis not as if I'll miss anything."

He nodded, getting to his feet as she did, and guiding her back along the paths. She trailed one hand through the water of the fountain as they passed, and he watched a little oddly as she did. Then they were at the doors, and he was ushering her inside.

He pulled the doors closed behind them. Reached for the lock, one that would have to be opened with a key.

"Donovan," she asked, and he paused, and turned to face her instead.

"Have you truly been alone all this time?"

He frowned. "I deal with others only when I'm forced to."

"Well, that's not exactly what I meant."

"What then?"

She lowered her gaze. "I...I mean...have you been... you know. Without a woman? All this time? An entire century?"

He blinked, gave his head a shake. "What odd questions you ask, Rachel," he said. "Why do you want to know?"

She shrugged, and realized she'd been breathlessly awaiting his answer. "I…perhaps I shouldn't have asked something so personal." She met his gaze, though, battling the turmoil in her belly. "But you did say you'd tell my anything I wanted to know."

"I did, didn't I?" His voice was no longer gentle. In fact he seemed angry. He gripped her arm, his touch careful, but firm and possessive, as he led her onward. And she noticed that he seemed to have forgotten all about locking that door.

But she wasn't sure what had replaced it in his mind, and that frightened her more than anything ever had.

Chapter 9

I knew what she was doing. Trying to get to me. Trying to make me feel something for her. Desire, and perhaps something more. Because if I did, I'd soften. I'd care. I'd let her go, despite the fact that it could cost me everything.

She was wrong, of course. I'd taught myself too well over the centuries I'd spent alone. I would not care. Not for her, nor anyone.

I did desire her. She'd succeeded in that regard. But not because of her clever ploys. I'd desired her from the moment I'd seen her again, grown into a beautiful woman, standing in the doorway of that pub and beckoning me inside.

I opened her chamber door, but didn't stand politely outside when she went in. Instead, I followed. And closed the door behind me.

She turned when she heard the thunk of the door banging shut, and her eyes widened, though she quickly tried to hide her alarm.

"You didn't tell me, Rachel. Why did you ask what you did?"

She lifted her chin. "I apologized for that," she said. "I was only curious."

"I think it was something more than that." I took a step toward her, but stopped when she backed away.

"I don't know what you mean."

"Yes, you do. You're playing a dangerous game, Rachel. Perhaps you don't realize how dangerous."

She shook her head. "I didn't mean—"

"Since you're so curious about sex, I'll tell you. It's very different, sex with a vampire."

Lowering her head, her cheeks flaming, she closed her eyes. "I don't want to hear this."

"You asked. You'll hear the answer. Look at me, Rachel."

Her jaw tight, she did as I asked. And I sent my will into her mind, took control, as easily this time as flicking a switch. "Come here."

She opened her mouth as if to refuse, then blinked in shock as her body disobeyed. Her feet, scuffing the floor, propelled her forward. "Closer," I told her, and she came. She stood very close to me. Head tipped back, eyes frightened, but aroused, glistening with a titillating mixture of fear and desire as she waited. And I knew why she responded this time when she hadn't before. Because it was what she wanted.

I lifted a hand to her face, touched her cheek very lightly, and trailed my fingers downward. Over her jaw, and chin, and then gently down her neck, pausing to feel the heady beat of her pulse there. Desire rushed through me. It wasn't supposed to. I hadn't planned it this way.

My fingers trailed lower, touching delicate collarbones, tracing her sternum, and then flitting lightly over one breast. I felt her response, the soft breath she drew, the tightening

of her nipple beneath my fingers. But more than that, I felt
my own reaction. She'd angered me...her power over me,
the danger that power represented. My own apparent inability to remain untouched by her, to resist her allure. I'd
meant to frighten her away, to show her how dangerous I
could be so she'd stop tempting me with her eyes, and her
words, and every damned breath she drew. Instead, I was
only making it worse.

"Please...."

It was a whisper, a plea. I drew my hand away, but my
fingertips tingled still. I wanted her.

"Playing on my desires is a risky game, Rachel," I told
her. "Because I can touch your mind with mine." I stared
down into her eyes. "Kiss me, Rachel."

She leaned up, her lips trembling, but parting, as they
touched mine. Then touched them again. I stood motionless
for a moment, but then shuddered and bowed over her,
taking her mouth, possessing it, invading it, as she pressed
her body tight to mine.

She tasted like honey. Her effect was like that of some
addictive drug, and my craving for her more powerful than
anything I'd ever known.

When I finally lifted my mouth away from hers, I was
breathless, my heart pounding. But hers was as well.

Drawing a steadying breath, I delivered the final lesson.
"Do you want to know the worst of it, Rachel? The bit of
knowledge that will frighten you the most?"

She nodded, only once.

"Even with this power, I couldn't make you do anything
you didn't truly want to do. Your will is too strong for
that." And with that, I released her, closed my mind off
again, broke the connection.

She stood there, staring at me, but the fire in her eyes
came as much, I thought, from anger as from the desire
that still lingered there.

"You...you bastard." It was a whisper.

"I thought I behaved with a great deal of restraint. I didn't want to, Rachel. I don't think you did either."

She looked away. "Are you enjoying this, Donovan? Trying to humiliate me?"

"I was only making a point. Don't try to seduce me into letting you go, Rachel. I won't be played that way. I won't be manipulated. I may desire you but I'll never care for you. Never. I'm incapable of it. But if you insist on arousing my desires, I won't be denied. I'll have you."

She glared at me, her eyes snapping with a fire I thought I'd extinguished by now. "If the only way you can have a woman is by taking control of her mind, then I pity you, Donovan O'Roark."

I opened my mouth to reply, only to find myself unable to find words.

"And if you think what you've accomplished is so impressive, you're a blind man." Without another word, she gripped the elastic waistband of her blouse and tugged it over her head. And then she stood there, breasts bared and perfect, plump and firm, swelling toward me like some forbidden fruit of Eden.

She moved closer to me. "Go on," she whispered. "Touch me." She gripped my hand, and drew it upward, pressing my palm to her breast. I closed my eyes as the warmth of her filled my hand. Air hissed through my teeth, and I felt the heat stirring, bubbling up inside me like a volcano, long dormant, about to erupt. I told myself to turn away, to leave the room, but I couldn't. My hand moved, caressed, squeezed. And then my other hand rose to do likewise, and my eyes fell closed as the desire became overwhelming.

Her breath stuttered out of her, her head tipping backward. Exposing her neck, satin-soft and utterly tempting.

Lying before me like an offering to a dark god. An offering I wanted to take.

"So you see?" she whispered. "This power you have over me...it isn't only you who wields it. I can as well. And if it was seduction I had on my mind, Donovan, I'd have done more than ask a simple question of you."

And with that she took a quick sharp step backward, away from me, and left me standing there, panting, aroused to a state near madness, wondering if she had a clue what she had done.

"You're a fool." I snagged her waist, and jerked her closer, one hand pushing her head backward as my mouth parted.

Her body crushed to mine, I bent over her and sank my teeth into her tender throat. She gasped, stiffened, but then as I suckled her, extracting the precious fluid from her body, she uncoiled. Her body melted in my arms, and her head fell back farther. She arched her neck, pushing against my mouth. "Yes," she whispered. "Oh, yessss..."

I drew away, not sated, only having sampled the barest taste of her...wanting more. Panting with wanting more.

Her hand stroked me, caressing the throbbing hardness between my legs, and in spite of myself, I arched against her touch. But I couldn't do this. Couldn't take her the way my body was screaming for me to do.

Because there was something more than desire here, something that frightened me. This entire demonstration of mine had backfired, hadn't it? She was the one who was supposed to be frightened.

I gazed down into her eyes, and knew she wasn't. Not really. Oh, there was some fear in her eyes, but it only served to enhance the wanting there.

As if she could see the indecision, my hesitation and my need to leave this room, she reached for the skirt, unfastened it, began to push it lower.

I closed my eyes, turning my back to her. "This…is not going to happen."

"You want it, too."

"Yes. I want to pierce your body with mine and take you. Just as I want to drain every drop of blood from your succulent throat, Rachel."

"You wouldn't hurt me."

I spun around. "What if hurting you is exactly what I want to do?"

"You don't." She shoved the skirt to the floor, stepped out of the panties, and came to me again, her hands sliding up the front of my shirt.

I gripped her wrists and stared down at her. Naked, aroused, all but begging me to take her. So aroused she barely knew what she was doing. I stilled her hands when she started unbuttoning my shirt. "Stop it, Rachel."

She froze, blinking up at me. When I released her hands she lowered them to her sides, and I noticed her trembling, head to toe.

She turned her back to me, and not knowing what else to do, I left the room.

What had she done?

Oh, God. Rachel flung herself onto the bed, hiding her face in the satin coverlet, battling tears of utter shame. "It was him," she muttered. "He *made* me behave that way. He…" But she knew it wasn't true. He hadn't forced anything on her. She'd acted on her own, except for that one brief interlude when he'd meant to demonstrate his alleged power over her. And she'd had to reciprocate—to salvage her pride by showing him that she had power, too. Feminine power to bend the man to *her* will.

And she had. Perhaps too much, because he'd lost control. She'd felt it, sensed it. And understood it because it had happened to her as well.

She'd behaved like a well-trained whore. Who *was* this woman in her body? Not her, not Rachel Sullivan. She'd never act that way with any man. Never.

But he wasn't any man. He was her guardian.

Wasn't he? What if she was wrong?

She had to get out of here. Now, tonight. She couldn't trust herself to remain near him, couldn't think straight this close to him. What was this thing she was feeling, this certainty that he was meant to be hers, now and forever? Was it foolishness? A childish dream?

She sat up slowly, wiping her eyes and scanning the room for her clothes. Heat flooded her face when she spied them thrown carelessly on the floor. She'd done that. Undressed for him, unashamed, brazen. No, it wasn't her, but some wild woman who'd been living silently inside her. Hiding, and choosing now to emerge—the worst possible time.

No, she had to leave. She tugged on her clothes, paced to the door and cracked it open, just slightly. He was nowhere in sight. But loud, crashing music came up from below—the great hall. Beethoven, she thought. Violent in its power.

She crept into the hall and toward the stairs, then down them only a bit. Just enough so she could see him in the great hall. He stood near the blazing hearth, head lowered, eyes closed. Utterly still as the music smashed over him.

Licking her dry lips, she moved lower, reaching the bottom of the stairs, not taking her eyes off him until she slipped around the corner. He never moved, never flinched, or even raised his head. She'd moved in near silence, but somehow she'd expected him to know. To be aware of her, as if crediting him with some sixth sense he couldn't possibly...

Or maybe he could. But he didn't notice her.

She'd planned to make her escape tomorrow while

he…slept. But she couldn't wait, not now. He was too confusing…and too angry at her for her feelings.

Her hand rose to touch the spot where he'd fed at her throat, and she felt the tiny wounds there. Not sore, but tingling with erotic awareness, so tender now, so sensitized. Just touching them reawakened the memory of his kiss, his touch…his mouth working her there.

She had to pause, lean back against a cool stone wall and draw deep breaths into her lungs. She wanted him. She desired a man she truly didn't know, though it felt as if she'd always known him. A vampire, but that made no difference to her.

She couldn't stay, because Lord only knew what she might do if she stayed. If he came to her room again, kissed her again…

But he wouldn't. He didn't want to care for her, he'd made that clear. Straightening, she squared her shoulders, and followed the corridor to the library. Then with one last glance behind her, to confirm he hadn't followed, she went inside. The French doors remained as they'd been before. Closed, but unlocked, and a moment later she was outside the castle. Free, in his beautiful garden of night.

For a moment she hesitated. It was such a contradiction, a man like him, having a place like this. As if he was capable of appreciating pure beauty. As if he had the soul of a poet, and not a determined hermit.

Shaking that thought away, she walked around the castle, each step faster than the one before, until at last she was running. Her hair blowing in the night wind as she pushed her muscles to their limits, racing through the darkness along the path, ever farther from the castle and toward the road that led to it. A road that meandered among woods, and later fields, and the village itself.

Free. She was free at last.

And that was when she heard the hounds.

Chapter 10

Hounds? She didn't understand. Not at first. But then she heard the men's voices in the distance, village men. And then the hounds drowned them out. Crying, baying in a horrific cacophony of noise that chilled her blood.

Marney Neal's hounds, she thought vaguely, knowing the animals were trained hunters. But they didn't hunt game, they hunted men. Marney trained them for that purpose. So if they were out tonight they must be after some criminal.

Then why were they heading toward the castle?

Donovan?

She swallowed hard, but her throat was dry. And then she stood there, frozen in fear, as the hounds rounded a curve in the road and came into sight. Running, bearing down on her. A horde of galloping, baying death. She whirled, panic taking hold as she surged into the woods, even knowing they'd offer no protection. But the dogs were too fast, too determined. One leapt, and his forelegs clawed her back, propelling her forward. Instinctively she rolled to her back, but the beast was upon her, teeth flashing. And then, suddenly the dog was hurled away.

Donovan. He stood above her, surrounded by the dogs, wielding a club as they lunged and snapped at him. "Go," he shouted. "Run for the castle. Go!" One snatched his arm in horrible teeth. She heard fabric tearing, saw blood as Donovan clubbed the animal uselessly.

Shaking, dirty and terrified, she struggled to her feet. And then she staggered toward the road. But she stopped as Donovan went down and the dogs leapt in for the kill. Screaming, she crouched low, scooping up hands full of debris and hurling it at their tawny bodies to get their attention.

"Here, you filthy beasts! Here! Come!" One dog turned toward her snarling. "Come for me then," she cried, and then she turned to run, knowing they'd follow.

And they did. She made it to the road with the hounds on her heels, now. But the men were in sight, and she cried out to them. "Marney Neal, call off your hounds! Call them off!"

"Sakes, 'tis Rachel!" someone said. But then the dogs were on her, knocking her down once more.

One of the men raced forward, shouting commands at the dogs. Thankfully, they were trained well enough to obey at once. The dogs fell away from her as one, and sat as docile as pups, awaiting the word of their master. And then Marney himself, beer on his breath, was leaning over her, helping her to her feet.

"Rachel, fer the love of God, where've ye been? We've been worried to death for you! Are you harmed, girl? Are you harmed?"

She let him help her to her feet. "What in the name of God were you thinking, turning those killers lose on me like that, Marney Neal! I should have you jailed!"

"Nay, 'twas for you I done it, child. You disappeared and we feared the murderin' O'Roark had taken you to his lair!"

"What utter foolishness!" She brushed the dirt and twigs from her clothes, and sent a furtive glance toward the woods where Donovan must still by lying. Perhaps dead, already.

"Is it, Rachel?" Marney eyed her suspiciously. "I take the hounds through these woods every night since that bastard has been in residence. Just to be sure he stays within his castle walls, and doesn't venture out to make victims of my neighbors."

"You're a superstitious fool. Donovan O'Roark is harmless."

"Then what are you doin' here wandering these godforsaken lands? And where have you been these past two nights, Rachel?"

She lifted her chin, met his eyes. "Had I agreed to wed you as you wanted, I'd feel that to be your business, Marney Neal, but since I turned you down I've nothing to say."

"You've been at the castle. As his lover?" he asked.

"As a guest, Marney. No more than that. Mary knows full well my interest in the legends associated with Donovan's ancestor. He's offered to help me with my research."

"Indeed!" Marney huffed, and eyed the castle as if it were something demonic. "Well, you're found now. Come with me, back to the village. Mary will be relieved to see you there, and well."

She glanced again toward the woods, then quickly at Marney again. "No. I'll return to the castle tonight. Tell Mary I'm fine and will contact her shortly."

He set his feet, hands on his hips. "I'll not have it."

"*You* have no say in it. Now kindly take your hounds and go home, Marney, before I decide to inform the authorities about this deadly pack you set on me. They nearly killed me. No doubt the law would see them all shot just to preserve the safety of the citizens.''

"You wouldn't—"

"I will, I swear on my mother's grave. Unless you leave now, I will.''

His eyes held hers only for a moment. Then lowered. "You've changed, Rachel Sullivan. The States have done this to ya, no doubt. Or perhaps 'twas that monster in the castle.''

"I've grown up. I won't have you or anyone running my life for me. Not anymore.''

"Fine. Ye deserve whatever fate befalls ye. But mark my words, Rachel, the man of that castle is no human bein'. He's a monster, and more dangerous to you than my dogs ever could be.''

He turned to go, with his dogs leaping up to follow, tails wagging. Harmless pets. Rachel waited until they were out of sight. Then she turned and ran back into the darkness of the trees, falling to her knees beside the dark shape on the ground.

"Donovan?"

He opened his eyes, his face pain-racked and pale in the night. "You could have gone with him," he whispered.

"Aye, I could have." She tore strips from her skirt and tied them tight round the wounds to stanch the bleeding. She'd never seen so much bleeding. "Can you stand? Walk?"

He tried to get up, faltered, and Rachel gripped him quickly, helping him to his feet. Then, pulling his arm around her shoulders, she propelled him forward, through the woods toward the castle. The road would be easier, but she'd prefer they not be seen by prying eyes. Especially Marney Neal's.

"There's a trail to the left," he managed, though he spoke through gritted teeth. "A shortcut.''

She took him that way, found the trail and followed it, but felt his eyes on her face. "Why?" he asked her, breathless, still bleeding.

"Don't ask foolish questions, Donovan O'Roark."

He leaned on her heavily, and when he spoke, his words were slurred. "Is it foolish to ask why? You were free. It's what you said you wanted."

"I wanted my freedom, yes," she said. "But not at the cost of your life." She shook her head. "You jumped into the midst of those hounds as if you thought yourself invincible. You could've been killed." He said nothing, and she tugged him faster. "Don't be telling me again how you can care for no one besides yourself, Donovan O'Roark, for 'tis a bald-faced lie an' you know it."

"No—"

"No? No, you say? Why, then, would you risk your own life to save mine?"

He shook his head. She couldn't see his face, because he kept it so low. Or perhaps he had no choice, too weak to hold it upright.

"You're no more selfish than you are a hermit," she said. "You're selfless, and more lonely than you even realize. An' I'll tolerate no more of your nonsensical lies. I've seen through this mask you wear, Donovan, and you can't don it again."

"You're seeing what you want to see."

Her hand felt damp, and she looked down to see the blood dripping from it where she clung to him. "Damnation, why do you bleed so?"

"It...it's part of what I am. Bleeding to death is one of the few ways I can die."

"That and sunlight," she whispered, glancing at the sky between the trees.

"There's plenty of time before dawn, Rachel. More's the

pity. It is only with the day sleep these wounds will heal. Until then—''

"Until then I'll stay beside you and be sure you don't bleed to death," she told him.

It shocked me. Astounded me, really. But that was precisely what she did.

My unwilling captive vanished, the rebel was gone. Her stubborn determination, her boundless energy, was directed toward helping me now, rather than escaping me. She eased me onto the settee in the great hall, then ran back toward the door. For the briefest of moments I thought she would run from me now that she'd seen me safely back to the castle. I was utterly bewildered when, instead, she turned the lock.

"What—"

"For Marney Neal and those narrow-minded fools like him," she said, back at my side now. "Those hounds were meant for you, not me, Donovan. You must know it. An' those men would have stood gladly by an' let them tear out your heart had it been you and not me on that road." She knelt on the floor beside me, shoving her hands through her hair, her cheeks pink with exertion, or frustration, or anger. "Lordy, how do you live like this?"

It wasn't a question she expected me to answer. Already she knelt beside the settee, tugging my shirt away to reveal the jagged tear in my side. Tearing the skirt she wore, until little remained but shreds, she packed the wound, and wrapped strips around my waist, tying them so tightly I could scarcely breathe. Her every touch brought on the most intense pain—and the most excruciating pleasure— I'd ever known. I thrilled at her hands on me, no matter the reason.

"Why do you come back here at all, Donovan," she

asked. "There must be places in the world where you're safe."

"There are." I looked around the hall, my gaze straying to the hearth where Dante and I used to sit and talk for hours on end, or read in companionable silence while the fire danced. "But this place is…dear to me."

"Then move it."

I only frowned at her.

"'Tis done all the time. Rich folk buying castles and having them moved stone by stone to the place of their choice."

I shook my head slowly. "It wouldn't be Ireland."

"No."

"You came back, Rachel. Despite the narrow-mindedness, despite the unwanted attentions…"

Her head came up sharply. "An' what would you know of that?"

"I know. Marney Neal would do well to know when to give up." I smiled slightly, despite the burning pain in my side. "Before you do him bodily harm."

"Aye, an' he's lucky I didn't tonight." She eyed my skin, shaking her head at all the blood. "You've watched me, haven't you?"

So she knew. I'd sensed it before. That she was aware somehow of my presence those nights when I'd drawn near to her, pulled as if by some irresistible force.

"There was a time, long ago," she whispered, dabbing now at the blood with a dry bit of crumpled fabric, "when I nearly drowned in the river near my home. Someone plucked me out, breathed into my lungs, and brought me back. But even as I lay there, choking, he vanished." She stopped wiping and met my eyes. "'Twas you, wasn't it?"

I lowered my head.

"And later, after my folks passed on. When I lay awake, frightened and alone, someone came to me in the darkness.

Just a dream, I thought when I was older. But 'twas no dream, was it, Donovan? 'Twas you, the man who told me he was my guardian angel, that I'd be safe, always.''

I released a long, slow breath. "It was."

"Did you ever know what that meant to me? Did you know how I slept soundly, how I believed it, how I clung to it? My parents were gone, but I had someone, still. Someone watching over me as my dear ma had, protecting me as my da had done. 'Twas the second time you saved me, you know.''

"No," I said. "I didn't know."

"Now you do. Quite a thing for a self-servin' monster to do, wasn't it, Donovan?"

"You don't understand," I began. But I wasn't certain I could explain. I didn't understand it either. Not fully.

"Make me understand then."

Nodding, I shifted to one side, so she could sit beside me on the edge of the settee. I saw her gaze shift quickly to the wound again, as if to assure herself my movement hadn't started the bleeding up again. "Dante told me of our nature, long ago. He told me that only certain mortals can become…what we are."

Her intense expression told him how interested she was in hearing more.

"As a mortal, I had a rare antigen in my blood. It's known as belladonna. That made me one of those few, one of the Chosen, as we call them."

"That's fascinating. I had no idea…"

"I know. Vampires are…aware of mortals with the antigen. We sense them, just as Dante sensed it in me. And there's more. There's a…a connection. For each vampire there's a mortal somewhere, one with the antigen, for whom that connection is stronger. So strong that we're drawn to them."

"And…were you that mortal for Dante?"

I nodded. "Yes. I never knew it, but he watched over me for most of my life. If trouble had come, he'd have protected me. And if I'd needed help, he'd have sensed it, wherever he might have been, and he'd have come."

She lowered her head, made a noise of disbelief in her throat.

"You don't believe me," I stated.

Slowly, she raised her eyes to mine. "If the legends are true, Donovan, he attacked you as you walked alone one night. He made you into what he was. If you call that protection, then—"

"I was dying."

She blinked fast. Her eyes widened.

"I didn't know it, of course, but Dante did. I'd been feeling the symptoms for weeks. Weakness, dizziness, blacking out for no reason. I had no idea what was wrong, and I'd thought it was something that would pass. But it wasn't."

"How do you know?"

I didn't answer that. Couldn't. Not yet. It would be too cruel to give her so much to deal with all at once. I couldn't tell her that mortals with the antigen always suffered the same fate—an early death. I'd been very close to my end.

"I simply do," I told her instead. "There's no doubt."

She stared down at me. "Then...you'd have died if he hadn't...done that to you."

"Without a doubt."

She nodded, deep in thought. "But he could have given you the choice. He never asked you to decide."

I smiled slightly, remembering. "Dante was never one to take time about acting. He was impulsive. Action first, thought later. But there were other reasons too. Had he told me, I likely would have repeated it to my parents, or the village priest. And some secrets simply must be kept, Rachel."

She drew my bloody shirt down over my body, deep in thought. I saw the moment she made the connection, because her eyes widened and met mine. "I have the antigen, don't I?"

I nodded. "You are the mortal I'm driven to watch over, Rachel. It's a part of who—of what I am. Don't go attaching any noble motivations to it. It's simply an irresistible urge. I couldn't ignore you if I tried."

"So saving me from the hounds…?"

"A reflex. Nothing more."

She lowered her eyes. "I'm not sure I believe you."

"Why not?"

She shrugged. "I think there's an element of choice involved, Donovan. You can't tell me that it was impossible for you to choose not to put yourself into the jaws of those hounds." She tilted her head to one side. "Or not to come back here at all. But you did. You came back because of me, didn't you, Donovan?"

I lowered my head. "Perhaps that was part of it. But I also came back because of Dante."

"Dante is dead."

"Yes. But I don't know where…"

Frowning, she studied me. "Where? Where he lies, you mean?"

Sighing, I absently ran one hand over the wound in my side. "When they came for us, put their torches to the castle walls, the sun was just beginning to rise. We had no choice but to run. Flames…devour our kind very quickly, you see. We both knew our only hope was to make for the relative shelter of the woods, where the sun's light wouldn't penetrate quite as quickly. And perhaps that would give us time to find shelter. A few minutes, at best, but perhaps enough." She nodded, urging me with her eyes to go on. "When we emerged, they were waiting. We could have stood and fought, and likely defeated them all."

"But…I thought there were dozens…"

I nodded. "We're very strong, Rachel. We could have fought, but the sun allowed no time. We had to run. They pursued us, though, and we had no choice but to split up. I ran in one direction, Dante in another. The mob…they went after him."

"And what happened to you?"

"I made it to the forest, and the hayfield beyond. I saved myself by burrowing deep into a haystack and remaining there until nightfall. It offered thin protection, but I survived. Weak, burned in many places, but I lived."

"And Dante didn't," she said softly.

"I returned to the castle ruins by night…for weeks. Knowing that's where he would look for me if he were alive. Even after I left the country, I came back periodically to wait for him here. I had the place rebuilt, just in case. But he never came. Now I only want to know where he died."

"Will you put a marker there?" she asked, her voice quiet.

"A garden," I told her. "Something as alive as he was."

"You loved him very much. Yet you claim you care for no one."

"I loved him," I said. "He was the last person I ever let myself care for. The lesson his death taught me was too hard won to forget."

I felt heavy. Tired.

"If you can't love," she asked, "then how can you live?"

"It isn't so hard."

She closed her eyes. "I'm like you," she said. "In more ways than I realized."

"How?"

But she only shook her head as I slipped into slumber.

Chapter 11

She didn't realize the time until he went still, and his eyes fell closed. It wasn't like death, this slumber of his. More like a very deep sleep.

She'd told him she was like him. Only now did she realize how much. She hadn't loved, either. With one exception. Since her parents had died there had been only one being she'd truly loved. And as she'd grown older, she'd convinced herself that love had only been a dream. But the love for that dream angel had remained.

And now she knew he was real. Her savior, her dream, was real.

And damp with his own blood, in torn, dirty clothes. He'd watched over her as a child. Taken care of her more than once. She could do no less for him.

But she could never tell him. He must never know how much she'd loved him in her youth. The fantasies she'd had. Because he was afraid of love. She'd never known anyone so afraid.

Slowly, Rachel got up off the settee, and headed to her own rooms. She found clean washcloths and soft towels, and fetched a basin of warm water. Then she returned to Donovan. He'd object to her caring for him this way if he were awake. But he wasn't awake.

She took off his shirt, moving him carefully, half afraid doing so would jar him awake, or worse, start him bleeding again. She eyed the bandaged wound. No red trickle emerged. Good. But her gaze slid slowly upward, over his flat belly, and muscled chest. His dark nipples intrigued her.

Her throat went dry. She looked away. Dipping the soft cloth into the water, squeezing it out, she pressed it to his skin. But she could feel him underneath it. Taut and hard. Masculinity was like an aura emanating from his flesh. Almost a scent, it drew her.

She leaned closer, over his chest, her face near enough so she could feel the heat rising from him and touching her. Closing her eyes, she inhaled deeply. And something stirred down in the pit of her belly. Something she knew, recognized, because she'd felt it before. Whenever this man was near her she felt it.

But she had no business feeling desire for a man incapable of feeling anything beyond desire in return.

She felt it all the same.

"God, help me," she whispered. "But I do want you, Donovan O'Roark." She closed her eyes, tried to get herself under control. Dipping the cloth in the now pink-tinted water, she squeezed it out again, and carefully took away her makeshift bandages from his wound, to clean it properly.

Then she squinted, dabbed the blood away, and looked again.

It...it was smaller.

It was shrinking. Amazed, she watched as, in slow motion, the wound's edges pulled together like some kind of experiment in time-lapse photography. It took several minutes, but bit by bit the skin seemed to regenerate. Leaving a pucker, and then even that smoothed itself out and faded away.

Blinking in shock, she washed the spot clean, searching for traces of the tear, but it was gone. Gone. In something like awe, she drew her fingers over the new, healthy skin. "It's unbelievable," she whispered, and flattened her palm against his warm flesh.

When his hand fell atop hers, she jumped and quickly looked up at his face. But his eyes remained closed, his breathing shallow, barely discernible. But his hand closed around hers in his sleep. A sleep in which he'd told her he was beyond responding to any stimulus.

He'd been wrong.

And now the hand of this man, who claimed he didn't need or want anyone in his life, clung to her own, and for the life of her, she wouldn't have taken hers away.

I woke to a feeling of warmth spread upon my chest. And then as my senses sharpened, I knew that warmth was her.

Rachel was on the floor, her legs curled beneath her, while her head rested upon my chest. Her lips…barely touching the bared skin of it. One arm spanned me, hand on my shoulder. Her other hand was tucked beneath her, held tightly in my own.

I flexed and relaxed my fingers, to confirm what seemed unlikely. But it was true. I was the one holding *her* hand like a lover. Not the other way around.

I couldn't lie like this…not for much longer. Her soft breaths whispering over my skin were driving me to the edge of madness. I was hungry. And she was too near. Too…

Her fingers spread on my shoulder, then kneaded like a

happy cat's claws. She moved her face, as if burrowing, only my chest didn't give, and her lips brushed over it like fire. The groan that rose up from the depths of me was a rumble. A warning. The same rumble one might hear from a volcano as the pressure within builds. An eruption was dangerously near.

She stirred, satin hair tickling my skin as she sat up, batting huge dark eyes at me, myopic until she blinked the sleep haze away and brought me into focus. Then she smiled.

"It healed," she told me.

"I told you it would."

"I know, but seeing it with my own eyes…'twas amazing, Donovan."

I nodded, trying to ignore the fresh-wakened glow in her cheeks and the moisture making her sleepy eyes gleam. The tousled hair. She must look just like this when she's been thoroughly satisfied by a skilled lover, I thought. Just like this.

I tried to sit up. She noticed, and got off me so I could, and I instantly regretted the loss of her so near. But when she got to her feet, it was to press her hands to the small of her back and arch. She grimaced, groaned and rubbed, so I realized she'd spent a horribly uncomfortable day on the floor when she'd had a bed fit for a queen only yards away. "Rachel, why on earth didn't you go to your room?"

She kept her hands where they were, fingers massaging herself. But her head came up fast. "An' leave you here by the front door, unconscious and unprotected? Not likely!"

I lowered my head. The smile that wanted to come to my lips was a dangerous one, I knew. No sense encouraging her foolish notions. "You'd already locked the door."

"Marney Neal could make quick work of that lock, and 'twouldn't be the first time."

I went still, sought her eyes, but she kept them averted. "You say that as if you know."

"Aye."

The bastard. "What lock was it he made quick work of, Rachel?"

"The one on my room at the pub. Eight years ago, before I left for the States."

Her voice didn't break at all. Mine would if I spoke again. It would break or emerge as the growl I felt building up. I'd kill the bastard. I'd rip out his heart and—

"You're lookin' rather murd'rous, Donovan," she said softly, studying my face. "An' truly, there's no need. Marney's a thorn in my side, but a harmless one. He'd never have gone so far if he hadn't had a wee bit too much ale. An' I daresay he sobered up some about the time I shoved him out my window."

I blinked, then slowly reached out, hooking one finger under her chin and tipping her head up so I could see her face. She seemed to be telling the truth. "You pushed him out your window?"

"'Twasn't hard. Marney didn't have much balance that night anyway, as I recall. So he kicks in my door and starts groping at me like a ruttin' buck, goin' on about marriage and love and other such nonsense. I simply turned so his back was to the window, and gave him a bit of a shove."

I couldn't help it. I smiled. "But your room is on the second floor."

"Aye. He broke his arm in two places when he landed. Good for him our main road isn't paved, wouldn't you say?"

I felt an odd feeling welling up for Rachel Sullivan, in the center of my chest.

"No man alive ever got so much as a kiss from me

without my consent, Donovan. 'Tis not something I'd tolerate.''

My gaze faltered. ''Are you trying now to take the blame for what I did before?''

''I'm only saying you spoke true when you said that if I hadn't wanted it to happen, it wouldn't have. And not only because I'd have prevented it, but because you would.''

I met her eyes, my own narrowing. ''Don't start again tonight crediting me with qualities I don't possess.''

She shrugged. ''I'm starving. Aren't y—'' She broke off there, bit her lip, and sent me a quick, hot glance. Her trembling hand shot to her neck, but the wounds there were gone now. Would have healed with the daylight. As if they'd never been there.

''Do you…would you…''

''Don't.'' I looked away, forcibly, from her tender throat. ''Why don't you go to your rooms, Rachel. You must want a shower, a change of clothes.''

''But…how do you get… What I mean is, where do you…?''

I looked at her again, unable to help myself. ''I don't kill, if that's what you're asking. I have stores. Cold, stale, sealed in plastic bags.'' I swallowed hard, as one of my hands rose up to stroke her hair, arranging it behind her shoulder. My fingers touched the soft skin there. Felt the pulse thudding endlessly, the river of her blood, flowing there. Warm, living blood.

''You…you drank from me…before.''

''I shouldn't have done that.''

''It was…'' She swallowed hard, but her eyes heated, and the flame singed me.

''It was ecstasy,'' I finished for her. ''I know. That's the danger, Rachel. That's the allure. What makes us so dangerous to you. You love it. You want it. You crave what could end in your own destruction.''

She lifted her chin. ''You'd never hurt me.''

''Don't be so sure of that, Rachel.'' I turned away.

''But I *am* sure of it,'' she said to my back. I'd been walking toward the kitchens, but I stopped then and stood motionless. ''Perhaps you're the one who needs convincin'.'' She moved forward very slowly. When she slid her palms slowly up the length of my back, curling her fingers on my shoulders, I stiffened, inhaled sharply. ''I'm not afraid of you, Donovan. I've no reason to be and you know it, I think. But you're afraid of me, aren't you?''

''Don't be a fool.''

''I'd only be a fool if I were askin' you to trust me,'' she said, and she moved her hands slowly, caressing my neck, fanning her fingers up into my hair. ''Or to love me. But I'm not, Donovan. I'm not askin' for anything like that.''

She was, she knew she was. All her life she'd dreamed of this man. He was meant for her, she knew that. Somewhere deep inside her, she'd always known. She'd never been with a man. Even believing her guardian angel, her immortal Donovan O'Roark to be a fantasy, she'd saved herself for him. Only for him.

He didn't turn, didn't speak.

She lowered her hands to her sides. Defeated. Maybe her dreams were as foolish as she'd once convinced herself they'd been. Maybe she'd been wrong after all.

''I'm sorry. I thought…I thought you wanted me, too.''

Turning away, she went to the stairs, climbed them slowly, and found the haven of the rooms he'd created for some fantasy woman—a woman he must have dreamed of. A woman he'd never let in.

* * *

I stood where I was for a full minute. No longer. I ached for her, craved her with a force beyond endurance. And she was right, I feared her too. She could destroy me, if I gave her the power.

I went to the foot of the stairs, gazing up them, wanting with everything in me to go after her. I wanted her. It wasn't love. It wasn't trust. It was only need…a need I knew she felt as well.

I put my foot on the first step. Closed my eyes, swallowed the trepidation welling up in my throat. Told myself this was a bad idea. Very bad. I took another step, and another. And I could hear the shower running now. In my mind, I could see her standing beneath it, wet and beautiful, utterly naked, mine for the taking.

What man alive would deny her?

"Not me," I whispered, and the words emerged deep and throaty. "No, not me."

I took the rest of the stairs by twos.

Chapter 12

Her door stood open...in invitation, I thought. Her clothes lay tattered on the floor, and I recalled the hounds surrounding her. The fear in her eyes. The courage that surged in spite of it.

My fingers fumbled with the trousers I wore, and I stepped out of them, and into the bathroom. Nothing between us now but the flimsy shower curtain. Her naked on one side, beneath the pounding spray. Me naked on the other.

Suddenly the water stopped flowing. Her fingers curled around the edge of the curtain, and it slid open. And then she stood there, still, silent. Wide eyes sliding up and down my body, before finally meeting mine, holding them.

She stepped out, one foot lifting over the edge of the tub, lowering to the floor, then the other. She didn't reach for the towels stacked nearby. Instead she merely stood there, head tilted back, eyes dark and stormy.

I stared back at her, drinking her in with my eyes. Water

beaded on her skin, her shoulders and arms. Her tight belly. Rivulets formed, trickling from her long, wet hair down over slick, perfect breasts. She waited. Up to me, I knew. But did she really think I could turn away now?

Reaching out, I touched her. Ran one hand slowly over her hair, and followed the water downward, absorbing it into my palm as I skimmed her delicate throat, her tender breast, her narrow waist and rounded hip. I tugged her closer. And she came so easily, at the merest nudge of my hand. She pressed her body to mine with a soft sigh, twining her arms around my neck and tilting her head back for my kiss.

I shuddered in reaction to the feel of her in my arms, wet and so warm, as I touched my mouth to hers. My arms closed tight around her, one hand cupping her buttocks while the other cradled her head. When her lips parted, I tasted heaven, and the fire inside me flared hotter. With my tongue, I delved inside, to touch and stroke hers. I felt her shaking. Warming until her flesh was hot against my hands. Feverish. I arched hard against her, and she pushed back. No hesitation, no shyness. My hands slid up and down her shower-damp body, unable to get enough of the feel of her as I fed from her mouth. She was sweet. And my mind floated away, until all that remained was sensation. Desire. And the taste of her. I moved my lips away, licking the moisture from her jaw, and her throat. She arched backward, and I slid lower, drinking every droplet from her skin, from her breast. Taking the hard little nipple into my mouth and suckling, gently at first, but harder when her hands tangled in my hair. Scraping and nipping with my teeth, making her whimper in need, a sound that added fuel to the fire.

I wanted her…all of her, everywhere. Lower, I moved, dropping to my knees and kissing the wet path down her belly, nuzzling my face in the nest of damp curls, and then pushing deeper. Parting her secret folds with my tongue, I tasted her, and she cried out, fists clenching in my hair and tugging it. Hurting me so deliciously that my knees nearly buckled. Then she stepped back, just a little, urging me upward again, until I was standing. Her arms encircled my neck, and she lifted herself. I helped her, clasping the backs of her thighs and lifting them, positioning them around my waist. I felt her, warm and ready, teasing at the very tip of me, and closed my eyes at the flash of desire that nearly blinded me. And then she lowered her body over mine, took me slowly, so slowly inside her. Deeper…and deeper still, and when I felt the resistance, wondered at it, she pushed harder. A soft gasp, a small sound of pain.

I went still. Throbbing inside her, feeling her body's tightness pressing around me, holding me, I closed my eyes and knew the secret she hadn't told me. The gift she'd just given me. "Rachel…"

"Shh," she whispered, and then she moved over me, lifting away, lowering again. Slowly, excruciatingly, her breasts sliding against my chest as she did, taut nipples caressing my skin.

Slowly, I told myself. *Gently.*

She nestled her head in the crook of my neck, kissed me there, suckled me there. Moved faster. Her breaths hot and quick on my skin. I pushed her back to the wall, gripped her buttocks and held her there, thrusting into her deeply, again and again.

She gasped, and clung to me, head thrown back, mouth open. I kissed her, took her mouth as I took her body, but the need wasn't sated. Even as my passion neared release, I knew it wouldn't be.

And it was as if she knew, sensed it somehow, because she clasped my head and drew it lower, pressed my face to her neck, tilted her chin upward, so the tender skin pressed to my lips. I felt the pulse pounding there, tasted the warmth and salt of her skin, knew it would be as good for her as for me, told myself there was no reason to deny what she offered.

"Take me, Donovan," she whispered. "Taste me…"

I shivered. I hungered. I neared release more with every thrust, and craved as I'd never craved before.

With a trembling sigh, I parted my lips, closed them over her thudding pulse and, quickly, pierced her throat. She drew a harsh breath, but her hands pushed my head closer, clung to me and she pressed her neck to my greedy mouth. And I fed. Suckled, devoured the very essence of her, and heard her short staccato cries as she neared climax. And then I heard nothing but the thunder of my own heart beating in time with hers as I exploded inside her. She screamed my name, shuddered around me, and slowly went limp in my arms.

I lifted my head, kissed the wound I'd left in her neck, and then her cheek, and her hair, and her lips.

She opened heavy-lidded eyes, and stared up at me. And something about that look made me realize the enormity of my mistake.

It wasn't simple desire I felt for her. Not need, not physical longing. I *felt* something for her. Something powerful and older than time. I always had.

I'd done it, then. I'd put the power to destroy me squarely into her hands. All that remained was to see what she would do with it.

But not now. Not yet.

As I lowered her gently to her feet, she stared up at me, and her deep green eyes gleamed like emeralds in moonlight. She whispered, "Come," and she took my hand. Drawing me with her back into the shower, turning on the water. Standing with me beneath the spray. She wrapped herself in my arms and kissed me. Lingeringly… almost…lovingly.

She couldn't tell him how she felt, wasn't sure there were words for it even if she tried. Completed, somehow. As if a goal she'd been striving for all her life had finally come within reach. As if the very essence of her had been touched, shared, poured out into another soul. She was happy, truly happy for the first time in her memory.

He didn't feel the same. Couldn't love her. Wouldn't trust her. But she refused to dwell on those things right now. There would be time. So much time.

She'd get her wish, her dream. The man she'd loved all her life. She lowered her eyes, tried to believe he would return that love. Eventually.

"What is it?" he whispered, stroking her hair as he held her. They'd moved from the shower to the bed, where they snuggled now like lovers. Tough to believe he felt nothing for her. Impossible, in fact.

She shook her head. "Nothing, Donovan. I was just thinking…"

"Thinking about what?"

Shrugging, she brushed away her doubts. "I'd like to walk outside," she told him. "In the moonlight."

"Were you always such a night person, Rachel?"

She smiled at him, ignoring the wariness, the uncertainty in his eyes. "'Tis growing on me." She sat up, sensing his growing discomfort with the intimacy of holding her in bed this way, now that the desire was spent. For her part, she'd have just as soon remained like that through the night, but…

She walked to the closet, pawed the clothes and chose carefully. A dress of white, so he couldn't help but focus on her out there in the darkness. With a full, soft skirt that would dance in the slightest breeze, and a plunging neckline to remind him of how much he still wanted her. She hoped.

"I've always wondered what lies beyond this fence of yours," she said as we walked side by side in the moonlit night. Her hair, dried during lovemaking and untouched by a comb, hung in natural, careless curls, giving her the look of a wild thing of the forests. A fairy, or a nymph. She enchanted me.

I should never have made love to her. Never.

"I can show you," I heard myself tell her.

"But…there's no gate."

Frowning, I tilted my head, watching her study the tall, sturdy fence. "And how do you know that, Rachel?"

She looked at me quickly, then averted her eyes. "I…used to come here. As a child."

"Often?"

Meeting my gaze, her own hooded, she shrugged. "As often as I could slip away. I knew 'twas you, even then, you see. My secret protector."

I lowered my head to hide my reaction to her words. My stomach clenched tight, twisted and pulled. "Do you still want to see inside?"

She nodded.

"Come here, then."

Frowning, she came closer. I scooped her up into my arms, bent at the knees, and leapt the tall fence. I heard her delighted squeak as I came down on the other side. And then she went silent, seemingly content to remain in my arms as she scanned the woods to her left, and the rolling meadow in which we stood. Well-worn paths meandered among the lush sweet grasses, and into the woodlot. "Look," I whispered, turning with her, pointing.

In the distance a doe lifted her head to glance our way briefly. Then she went back to nibbling. "Donovan, there. Beyond the doe," Rachel whispered.

"Yes," I said, "I see them." Twin fawns frolicked in the deep grasses. Gently, I set Rachel on her feet. "The fence keeps hunters—men like Marney Neal and his hounds—away. The deer can leap the fence easily though. Come and go as they please. Most of them seem content to stay here.''

"So you've made a haven for the deer.'' She continued watching, laughing softly, a sound more disturbingly beautiful than a night bird's song, at the twins' antics.

"Not only the deer.'' I turned toward the fence, crouching low and pushing the deep grasses aside. "There are hidden places like this one, where the smaller creatures can get underneath. And the game birds fly over to find safety. Come,'' I said, extending my hand. Her delight in this place so pleased me, I couldn't resist showing her more.

When she closed her hand around mine, a feeling of warmth suffused me. And for a moment, it seemed perfect, natural. Until I reminded myself that it was fleeting. She'd leave here, one day soon.

I led her over the meadow, to the place where wildflowers spread like a patchwork carpet in every direction. And beyond that, to the pond, fed by two streams. It glittered in the moonlight. Geese swam on the silvery water, undisturbed by our intrusion. Rachel sank into the grass on the pond's bank, and in spite of myself, I sat down beside her. Closer than I needed to, and yet not close enough.

"It's as if they know you're no threat to them.''

"They should,'' I told her. "They've been safe here for generations.''

I felt her eyes on me. "Why, Donovan?''

I shrugged. "Why not?''

"Tell me.''

I looked at her, half reclining now. Like a goddess in her paradise. "All right,'' I said softly. "I created this haven for the animals because I understand them.'' I looked again at the geese, who swam further from shore as a fox came slinking slowly to the water's edge for a sip. "I know how it feels to be hunted," I told her.

I met her eyes. She nodded as if she understood. But she couldn't. Or…I refused to believe she could.

"You're truly a special man, Donovan O'Roark."

I shook my head slowly, but as she curled into the cradle of my arm and rested her head upon my shoulder, I *felt* special. Cherished.

God, I was a fool to feel the things she made me feel.

We stayed there, in my own private paradise for most of the night. Walking hand in hand, spotting and observing the wildlife. Like young mortals in love. Like some idealistic fantasy. And I relished every moment of it, in spite of the knowledge that doing so was a fool's dream. I only suggested we return to the castle when I knew dawn was on the rise, and Rachel still hadn't eaten.

But when we entered through the library doors, it was to the sound of urgent pounding, and shouts from the front. And even before I went to the great hall to answer the noisy summons, I sensed my brief time in paradise was coming to an end.

Mary O'Mallory stood at the door, breathless, red in the face. Her frantic gaze slid from me to Rachel, then relaxed slightly in relief. "Rachel," she sighed. "Lordy, girl, what took you so long?"

Rachel frowned, ushering her inside, one arm supporting the woman, and I knew she cared for Mary. Genuinely cared. I saw the worry in her eyes. "We were outside," Rachel explained. "Come, sit down before you faint dead away. Whatever is the matter?"

Mary sat, though on the edge of the settee. As if ready to spring and run should the need arise. "I need to speak with you, Rachel. Alone." She slid a sideways glance toward me, and I knew what she thought of me. That I was a monster. They all believed that.

All...except for Rachel. She'd never seen me that way, had she?

"There's nothing you can't say to me in front of Donovan."

Mary pursed her lips.

"He's my friend, Mary."

"Never mind. I'll give you your privacy," I offered. But I slanted a long look Rachel's way. Would she run now? Should I lock the door?

No. No need sending Mary into a panic. They wouldn't be long.

"I'll call you when we've finished," Rachel said. And I knew it was her way of promising she wouldn't run off. But she would, eventually. It was inevitable. And it was going to hurt.

I only nodded and left the two alone.

Rachel sat beside Mary and clasped the older woman's hands. "Now tell me, what's wrong?"

"The very fact that yer here, with that...that—"

"He's a man, Mary. Just a man. And he's been nothing but kind to me."

"Lordy, child, tell me you're not in love with him!"

Rachel only lowered her eyes. "Why don't you simply tell me why you've come."

"'Tis the villagers, girl. Marney Neal, above all. He's stirred them up until I fear history is about to repeat itself. An' I want you safe away from this place before it does."

A bird of panic took wing in Rachel's chest. "What are you saying?"

"Marney claims the beast has you under some sort of spell, child. That you're his prisoner, but too enchanted to realize it. He's convinced them you're in need of rescue, Rachel, and even now the men are gathering at the pub. 'Twas all I could do to slip away unnoticed, to warn you."

Rachel lowered her head, closed her eyes. "So they'll come here."

"Aye," Mary said. "An' I fear violence will be done this night, child. Ye must come away with me now."

Facing her squarely, Rachel nodded. "I'll come. But I'll speak with Donovan first."

"Rachel, you mustn't—"

"I must. I can't leave him here, unprepared. Unwarned. I can't go without telling him goodbye or explaining... No, you go on. I'll be along shortly, I promise."

Mary looked as if she were about to argue, but when she met Rachel's eyes, she seemed to change her mind. "I can see you're determined. What's between you two, Rachel?"

"Nothing that need concern you. Go, now. Try to hold the men off until I get there."

Sighing, Mary left. Rachel stood at the door, watching her go. Then she turned, wandered back to the hall that led to the library, and called Donovan's name. She heard his steps coming toward her, felt his essence touching her even before he came into sight. He only looked into her eyes, standing very still, then nodded. "You're leaving tonight, aren't you Rachel?"

"I must. You have to let me go, Donovan. It's—"

He held up a hand. "I won't stop you. My... arrangements are in place, for the most part. I can leave here right after you do."

She tilted her head, frowning hard at him. "My God, Donovan, do you still believe that's necessary? After what we've shared? The way we've talked...you really think I'd leave here only to tell your secrets to the world?"

He lowered his head. "What I believe," he whispered, "is that I'm as big a fool as Dante was. But I've no wish to suffer the same fate."

She looked up at him, stared deeply into his eyes, and

what she saw there was pain. "If you leave…I'll never be able to find you again. Will I?"

He averted his eyes. "That's the entire point."

"No," she said softly. "It's not even close to the point."

"Then what is?"

She stepped closer, gripped the front of his shirt in trembling fists. "Must I throw my heart at your feet and wait for you to kick it aside? I will then. You mean more to me than my pride."

"Don't, Rachel—"

"I love you, Donovan O'Roark. I've loved you all my life, and I will until I die."

His face seemed to crumple in pain.

"I'm leavin' you tonight, yes. Because I must. But only tonight. I'd have come back. I'd have come back here, for you."

"Rachel…"

"You'd do well to leave, too, Donovan, for there's danger to you here tonight. But it's up to you where you go. Far away, where I can never set eyes on you again. Or close by…close enough so that I can find you…or you can find me."

Slowly, he shook his head. "You don't understand. It's the curse of my kind to live our lives alone, Rachel. It's how it has to be."

"No. 'Tis how you've made it. You have a choice now, Donovan. But it's up to you." Tears choked her. God, she didn't want to leave him. To lose him. To never see him again. But if she didn't, she might lose him anyway. To an angry mob, just the way he'd lost Dante. Impulsively, tears streaming over her cheeks, she pressed her lips to his, clung to his neck for a brief, passionate kiss. Then she turned and fled, through the front door and into the waning night.

Chapter 13

When she left it was as if my heart had been torn apart. I should leave as well, I knew. I should pack up the few belongings I'd need, and make my way out of here. I didn't know what Mary had told her, but I didn't disbelieve Rachel when she said I'd be in danger here tonight. I should hurry.

I should. But I couldn't.

She said she'd come back, and damn me for a fool, I believed her. More than that, I wanted it to be true. This place had never been more alive—*I'd* never been more alive—than when she was here. Lighting my darkness. A blazing sun shining her warmth on my endless night.

She might betray me, as I'd spent so much time convincing myself she would. If she did, I'd be damned. But I couldn't leave until I knew.

I went to the settee, lowered myself to it, bowed my head, and sat there, very still.

Who was I kidding? She wasn't going to betray me. I'd

lost my heart to the woman, and when she came back I'd be here waiting. And I'd tell her, at last. My heart was in her hands.

Rachel sailed into the pub as if she hadn't a care in the world, though her heart was heavy. He'd be gone when she went back. He'd be gone, and she'd never see him again.

Still, she feigned surprise when she saw the men crowding the room, with Marney standing at the front of them all. "My," she whispered. "Business is better when I'm away, isn't it? And what's the celebration tonight that has half the village in attendance?"

"'Tis no celebration, Rachel." Marney stepped forward, clutching her hands as if she were his property. "But 'tis glad I am that you've returned. You'll be out of harm's way when we storm that damnable castle."

She frowned, and drew her hands from his. "An' why is it you're plannin' to attack an empty ruin?"

"Empty?"

"Aye," she said with a nod. "Donovan has gone. Only came for one last look at the place before leaving it for good. 'Tis a shame you didn't make him feel more welcome here, you know. He's a kind man."

"He's a beast!" someone yelled.

"Oh, I don't think that's true. He was kind enough to help me with my research before he went on his way." She walked behind the bar, reaching for her apron.

"I think you're lyin', Rachel," Marney said, eyeing her. "I think you're trying to protect him, an' you wouldn't be if you weren't under his spell."

"Spell?" she asked, wide-eyed. "Don't tell me you're fool enough to believe he's more than just an ordinary man?"

"You know he is."

She did. He was above and beyond ordinary and ten

times the man of any in this room. But instead of telling them so, she only shrugged. "I know no such thing. But I do know this, Marney. I'll not allow you to harm him."

"Then he *is* still there!" Marney shouted, banging a fist on the table.

"I didn't say—"

"You didn't have to. You've been naught but cold to me since your return, Rachel. An' everyone knows you'd planned to marry me before you left. 'Tis that beast who's swayed yer mind."

"I never planned to marry you. The plans were all on your side," she told him. "And 'twas indeed a beast who made up my mind, Marney, but the beast was you. Not Donovan O'Roark."

"We're goin' up there, and when we leave there'll be nothing left but rubble. He'll not escape us...not alive, at least."

He turned and the other men rose. They piled out the door, Marney leading them. Rachel surged after them all, but they moved quickly, and though she caught hold of several of the men, tugging at them, pleading with them, they were too frenzied to listen to her. When they turned onto the curving castle road, Rachel ducked into the woods and raced for the shortcut Dante had shown her, so she could come out ahead of them.

But when she got to the frenzied men again, it was to see the castle door opening to their pounding summons, and Donovan stepping out.

He eyed the crowd, shook his head slowly. He looked utterly calm, but she knew what he must be thinking. That she'd done this to him, just as her ancestor had done to his best friend. That she'd left him only to lead this crowd back here. That she'd betrayed him.

Then he lifted his head. "Where is Rachel?" he asked. "Have you harmed her?"

She blinked in surprise, unable to speak. He thought they'd harmed her? Then…

"Rachel's no longer your concern," Marney told him. "We all know you've bewitched her somehow, or she'd never defend you the way she has. Once you're gone, she'll be fine again."

"Defended me, did she? I'm not surprised," Donovan said, and she could have sworn he battled a gentle smile. "Once I'm gone, you say," Donovan went on. "So you intend to kill me, do you?"

"Aye," Marney growled.

"Just so long as you're honest about your reasons," Donovan went on. "You want me gone because of Rachel. Because it's me she loves and not you."

The men grumbled, and someone yelled, "Is that true, Marney?"

"So will you drive me out into the sunrise, Neal," Donovan went on, "or simply kill me here and now?"

"Here and now," Marney whispered.

"Are you sure you can?"

Marney's eyes narrowed and he lifted his rifle. Rachel screamed and lunged from the woods, slamming her body into Marney's, and groping for the gun. But she never found a hold. Marney staggered backward under the weight of her assault, and the shot cracked so loudly her eardrums split. Then she felt the burn…the heat. The rapid pulse of life from her body.

Blinking in shock, she would have fallen to the ground, had not Donovan lunged forward to gather her into his arms. "Damn you!" he shouted. "Damn you, look what you've done! Rachel? Rachel!"

She opened her eyes, studied his face. Then she turned to Marney. "Go," she told him. "Go away. If I see you again…."

Marney backed away. Already the other men were scattering, shocked from their fury, perhaps, to realize just what they'd been about to do. What had happened as a result of their foolishness.

Cradling her in his arms, Donovan bent over her, kissed her face. And Mary crowded through the retreating men, made her way forward while Marney stood in the road, blinking in shock. She leaned over Rachel, parting her blouse, and looking at her chest, where the pain throbbed and burned. Grimly, Mary lifted her gaze to Donovan's. "You can help her," she whispered. "Can't you?"

Through her fading vision, Rachel saw him nod. Then Mary turned away. "'Tis only a flesh wound," she called to Marney. "But I vow unless ye leave here now I'll inform the authorities an' have you arrested for attempted murder. An' if you ever bother these people again, I'll do it. Now go!"

Nodding, muttering that it wasn't his fault, Marney turned and ran away like the coward he was.

Mary faced the two of them once more. "I don't imagine I'll see you again, will I?"

Rachel said nothing, unsure what Mary meant.

"Goodbye, child. Be happy."

Then she was gone.

Rachel stared up into Donovan's eyes. "I was afraid you'd think I brought them…"

"I knew better."

"Did you?"

"You know I did. I kept telling you I couldn't trust, couldn't care…even when I already did. I doubted you, Rachel, from the start, and I'm more sorry than I can tell you. You didn't deserve that. But you never gave up on me, did you?"

"How could I? You're in my soul, Donovan O'Roark. You have been since I was but a wee girl."

"And you in mine," he told her. "You made me believe

in you, Rachel. Made me...made me love when I'd vowed it was something I'd never do. I love you, Rachel Sullivan. Do you hear me? I love you."

"Of course you do," she whispered. "You always have."

He smiled very gently.

"I'm dying," she whispered.

"Yes."

"But you can prevent it, can't you, Donovan? You can make me...like you."

"'Tis not an easy way to live, child. Never again to see the sunlight. Always knowing there are those who would hunt you, kill you simply for being what you are."

"Wandering hand in hand beneath the moonlight, spending every moment in your arms," she said weakly. "'Tis the life I want, so long as I can live it by your side. That's the dream I've always had, Donovan. To be with you...as we're meant to be...together."

"Then together we shall be, Rachel. Always." He lowered his head and kissed her, and she knew she'd found her dream come true, at last.

* * * * *

my gaze, Rachel McInnes," said me low when I bowed
It was something I'd regret that I never had. Rachel Sullivan.
Don't move me. I love you.

"I guess you do," she said urgently. "You aren't
him."

He smiled sweetly and—
"I'm through," she whispered.

Barry was pinned up, and I was the answer. You can
make me take you.

"We're in our way to live, child. Never again to see
the sunlight. Always knowing there are those who would
hunt you, but you simply for being what you are."

We came upon a land beneath the moonlight, grateful
my wary smile set in your breast," she said wearily. "It's
the last supper I had as long as he saw you nice. Then a
he drained by slumber, and I'm over to be with you, as
we're as it is," I asked.

Then I took one smiling figure. And low," He love
cool as he held and kissed her, and she knew she'd found her
own love, there too, at last.

MARRIED BY DAWN

Marilyn Tracy

Books by Marilyn Tracy

Silhouette Intimate Moments

Chapter 1

Gavin Deveroux stood outside the doors leading to the hotel's elegant solarium, hesitant for no reason he could discern. Beyond the doors lay an assignment he'd been commissioned to complete. Behind him lay decades of adherence to similar missions, comparable tasks—pleasurable or otherwise.

This particular mission seemed as straightforward as any other, though the cause for it remained slightly perplexing. A mortal had issued a challenge to the High Council, had practically dared the Society to come after her. A foolish and futile challenge, not even worth the time it would take him to dispatch the mortal.

And still he paused, more warily than in uncertainty, a stirring of unease rippling through him.

Voices from those attending the memorial service wafted through the doors. Memories from a time long ago danced across his mind, recollections that were drained of life,

faded with time and his Crossing into the Society. The last
memorial service he'd attended of any kind had been more
than two centuries before. And that had been his own.

And, perhaps because he was back in this city again, he
naturally thought of Jonathan, whom he'd last seen here.
Jonathan who had forsworn his place on the Council, who
had been banished from the Society altogether because of
his reckless love for the woman remembered tonight.

If there was one thing he'd learned in his years outside
mortal existence, it was that sooner or later everything returned to its starting place. What seemed a wandering, tor-
tuous path was, in the end, revealed to be only a circle,
with no beginning and no end. The simple fact that he was
here again, brought by the sister of the woman who had so
thoroughly changed the lives of everyone within the confines of the Society, seemed fitting, a return to the starting
place.

A single trill of husky laughter drifted through the doorway. As its resonance washed over him, Gavin understood
why he'd hesitated and, perhaps, why he'd thought of Jonathan.

The contralto laugh played on his skin like the brush of
a bird's soft wing. A warning, a beckoning. It hummed,
teasing the back of his mind, calling forth images long re-
pressed, willfully, thankfully put to rest lifetimes ago.

The laughing voice was no louder than any emanating
from the solarium, but unerringly he separated it from all
others, isolating it, frowning over it.

The contralto laugh was loosed a second time. Gavin
closed his eyes, allowing himself to thoroughly absorb the
cellolike sound. He felt his own lips curve into a smile.

A dark smile.

He and his kind laughed, to be sure, but never with such

a simplicity. A sharp, almost painful desire coursed through him and he opened his eyes, catching his breath in the empty hallway as if he'd been underwater and near drowning.

The strange moment passed as the echo of the laugh dissipated and he felt himself once again.

He would take the woman who had laughed so musically, so incongruously. She would be his reward once his objective was successfully attained. Against the intent of the rules, perhaps, but not expressly forbidden.

The Council knew it was always painful to be openly among those not of his kind, because the sensations felt among them were fiercely demanding and dangerous. And every member of the Society knew all too well the allure of the mortal race. Each of them, once upon a distant time, had tasted the mortal's brief desires, aches and longings. Once, yes, but those frail and bittersweet passions were nearly forgotten now by all, even the newest members. Almost forgotten.

Gavin heard the woman chuckle, and though it didn't convey quite the same feeling as her laugh, he was acutely aware of the same throaty, fully accepting quality.

Ahhh. Yes, she would be his reward…a woman who could laugh during a memorial service. She would take the sting of the mission from his heart, for the mission reminded him of Jonathan, whom he'd helped to banish from the Society.

This woman's laughter would be the balm to the wound in his soul, if he even still possessed such an encumbrance. To capture such a sound would ease the discomfort he still felt when he thought of Jonathan's madness.

He shook his hair back from his face as if shaking off the notion that he had any sort of wound. But he was filled with longing for the laughter of the faceless woman. She would feel so sweet in his arms.

With his acute sensory perception, he knew her exact location on the far side of the room beyond the doors that would lead him to her. This melodious woman would beg to give him her laughter even as he took it inside him forever, silencing that strangely alluring strand of music.

He found himself frowning at the notion.

Gavin forced another smile to his full lips. He knew it didn't light his eyes; it couldn't brighten him at all. Nothing could. He'd died years before, his soul damned even before that time. Glamour, riches, and eternal youth, he possessed all that his kind could ever want.

There were pleasures, this side of the Crossing. Many, many pleasures. And with the thought of the pleasure in taking the laughing woman uppermost in his mind, he crossed the threshold into the solarium.

His eyes scanned the crowd to find the Society's challenger, his target, amongst the mourners who'd had a year to lay their grief aside. And he sought his reward.

He found them both in a single glance.

Tara Michaels' laughter died away as her companion suddenly broke off the funny story he'd been telling her, gripped her arm and pulled her aside. She could smell the sour scent of his fear and excitement as he leaned close to whisper to her.

"Over there." He jutted his chin at the stranger walking in the door. "The very devil himself."

Every muscle in her body stiffened as she focused on the latecomer and she shook her head in instinctive negation.

If being the "very devil" meant being arrogant, smooth

and undeniably attractive, the newcomer fit the bill. Nothing about his persona was understated. He was dressed in loose-fitting slacks and a black French-styled peasant shirt—collarless and opened at the breast with a loosely strung drawstring. He'd rolled his shirtsleeves to the elbow, revealing muscular forearms that tapered to long hands and strong fingers.

He was the very picture of an artistic rebel, though his shirt was obviously made of silk, his shoes were expensive loafers and his longish honey-gold hair fell naturally in loose and free waves.

Without taking her eyes from him, Tara sensed that every woman in the room had turned to look at the new arrival. A slight hush fell over the crowd.

"That can't be Gavin Deveroux," Tara murmured, aching for Tom to point at someone else, wanting to cling to her instinctive denial. But even as the words left her mouth, she remembered that Tom had seen him before. The night her sister Charlene had been murdered.

The man Tom claimed wasn't even human shifted his gaze to hers as if he'd known ahead of time exactly where she would be standing.

She shivered at the thought and raised her chin a notch in defiance of him.

His eyes were hazel, she thought, a strange muddied green that seemed to catch the light from the chandeliers and turn dark golden. His gaze carried a detachment, a hint of flint-hard, knowledgeable desire.

His gaze flicked over to Tom and then back to her and she saw some lightning-quick understanding of who she was leap in his eyes like a blaze. Something in his gaze seemed to alter, brightening his unusual eyes and, at the same time, focusing some undefinable element of attention.

And she understood on some atavistic level that where he'd been conscious of her before, he was wholly and utterly aware of her now.

As aware as she was of him.

She was also aware that he was walking toward her. Slowly. Deliberately. The people standing around the solarium parted for him as grass might part to a scythe.

Tara felt as though all the air in the large chamber had mysteriously disappeared. She struggled to draw a breath. He gazed at her as if she were the only woman in the room, possibly the only woman in the world.

Tom was right, she thought, no longer resenting his fierce grip on her arm, but instead feeling grateful for the simple human contact. *Tom was right about it all: that Charlene's friends would be able to attend a memorial service if held in their place of work; that access to the airport in Las Vegas would make it easier for Gavin Deveroux to attend, thus easier for her and Tom to trap him. And, most of all, that this man is not human.*

She fought the power emanating from the stranger, battling the odd desire that rose in her at his intimate, demanding stare.

"Don't meet his eyes," Tom warned.

It was far too late for such counsel.

"I've told you what he's capable of doing. Remember what he did to Charlene."

She knew. She remembered and was sickened by it. This gathering in the softly lit solarium was in memory of her murdered sister, and still she couldn't drag her eyes from the stranger's.

Aside from Tom, she was probably the only other person in the room who had any idea just how dangerous Gavin

Deveroux was. And she was very likely one of the few people in the city who had an inkling of *what* he was.

She was inordinately relieved when he slowed his steps and then stopped altogether. Standing perfectly still, he smiled slightly, wholly at ease, only some ten feet away from her. Teasing her, she thought. Or taunting her.

She forced her gaze from his, picking up the first thing she saw, which happened to be the eulogy for her sister. She deliberately kept her unseeing eyes on the page, though the printed words swam before her. Finally the sentences on the page coalesced into some semblance of order. She nodded, as though Tom had asked her something.

"I'm ready," she said softly.

Tom leaned closer to her. She turned her head away, slightly sickened by the smell of hatred on his breath, pretending it was to hear him better.

"Remember, Tara. Whatever it takes. You've got to do *whatever* it takes to get him into that hotel room. Just until dawn. That's all. Signal me. And I'll do the rest—all the rest. You'll be able to do that much, won't you?"

"I will," she murmured, her eyes darting to where Gavin Deveroux stood, his gaze still on her. "Whatever it takes," she repeated faintly.

"It'll be easy for you to lure him into our trap. Can't you see how he's looking at you? He wants you. Everyone here can see that."

Tara couldn't say anything. The man's—the *creature's*—interest in her was palpable, like another presence in the room.

"You'll have your revenge for Charlene," Tom whispered.

Tara shivered. The man who stared at her so hungrily, so hauntingly, was the same evil being who had murdered her only sister. She had to keep telling herself that so she wouldn't turn and run from the room, from the city, from all the horror of the past year.

"For Charlene," she echoed, though she wasn't sure it was true. Wasn't she really doing this for Tom, because this creature had stolen his fiancée from him? And wasn't there a darker reason, one she didn't want to admit even to herself. She needed to punish—kill—Charlene's murderer, because this creature had killed the one person she'd never valued enough when she'd had her. When Charlene had run to Las Vegas, taking her place in a chorus line, abandoning all dreams of classical dancing, Tara had felt abandoned herself, that all her support and nurturing had been rejected. But who had really rejected whom?

"Ready?" Tom asked. "Just don't think about the danger. I'll be there to wipe the demon out once and for all. Just remember the signal."

For a moment, Tara knew a wild and unfettered terror. What was she thinking of? Murder? Destruction of another living creature? She couldn't do it. She was an English teacher, for heaven's sake, more suited to marking papers than marking another being's destiny.

"Tom...I don't think I can—"

She heard Tom inhale with a sharp hiss, before he growled with scarcely banked fury, "It's too late for doubts, Tara. You've got to do it. For Charlene. For every woman like Charlene. You and I can do something about him, about his kind. You want another woman's death on your conscience, Tara? Back down now and that's what you'll be doing. Condemning another woman to be beaten and ripped apart as Charlene was. Do you want that, Tara? Do you?"

Tara didn't answer his angry questions, but they served

to steady her once more. She squared her shoulders and stepped away from Tom. She had always believed that the pen was mightier than the sword, but sometimes, in the name of justice and retribution, even an English teacher had to wield a sword.

She walked to the lectern that had been placed on a flower-decorated dais. The room fell silent as she laid the eulogy on the polished stand and placed her hands on either side of its open pages.

"Thank you all for coming tonight," she said. "Perhaps it's strange to have this service a full year after Charlene's tragic death. Yet, now that all the investigations are concluded, perhaps we can focus on the joy we all felt in knowing her, rather than on the cruel reality and circumstances of her passing. She tried smiling, but the smile faltered as her eyes traveled across to Gavin Deveroux.

It had been Tom's idea to invite Deveroux to the service. *"He'll come if we let them know that Charlene wrote about their kind in her diary. And let him know where he can get it. Tell him she left a little something for him."*

"But I didn't believe in what she said...why should they think anyone else would?"

"They'll believe. Just like you do now. They wouldn't dare let their precious secrets out."

"But what if they send someone else?"

"They won't. Charlene mentioned Deveroux specifically in the diary. And you forget, I saw him."

Tom, a self-proclaimed authority in antiquities, had spent months researching archaic tomes to discover just how to approach the Council, a secret group that Tara had never heard of, or even dreamed existed before Charlene's death. Tom had made it his business to know because it was a

member of that strange Society that had left Charlene dead
and battered in his helpless hands.

And he'd taught Tara all he knew about the creature and
his kind. And over the months of providing proofs and his
relentless talking to her, he'd finally convinced her that the
impossible was possible, that the fantasy was all too terribly
real.

Now, however, standing among Charlene's friends and
co-workers, all she could feel was the dreadful irony of
having her sister's murderer—who'd left his devil's marks
upon her torn neck—attending this long-delayed memorial
service.

Once again her eyes were drawn unwillingly to Gavin
Deveroux. He nodded to her, as if acknowledging her
thoughts. As if admitting his guilt. *Yes, I killed your sister.
What can you possibly do about it?* His lips curved into a
smile of cruel satisfaction that belied the longing burning
in his eyes. Or was there something else in that smile,
something sweeter? She'd thought it was cruelty, but...

Tara felt a slow flush of anger and something else, something oddly akin to desire, work up her body and settle on
her face.

"We're here to remember my sister, Charlene Michaels," she said and her voice broke, not from grief but
from the sharp reaction she was experiencing to the presence of Gavin Deveroux.

The monster's gaze was still fixed on her, the enigmatic
smile still playing around his lips. The creature had the
audacity to smile at her at this solemn moment, when she
was asking her friends to remember their grief. He was
watching her with an intense, disturbing hunger in his eyes.
She wanted to scream at him. To jump from the stage and

slap his face, to run a silver dagger through him over and over again. Or better yet…a wooden stake.

Instead, baffling her, she felt a strange, comforting warmth passing from him to her, and her lips slowly curving upward in a grateful, acknowledging smile.

Dear God, she thought. She wanted the man who murdered her sister.

Chapter 2

Gavin watched the woman with the chestnut hair and hazel eyes. She was the antithesis of everything he knew, everything his world embraced. His head reeled with the realization that the woman he had to destroy was the very woman he wanted to claim as his prize.

His task was to end her life, swiftly and surely, but his other wish was to take her, to savor and possess her. A contradiction, an impossibility; he could not do both and still comply with the Council's demands. But knowing this did nothing to assuage his desire.

This Tara Michaels embodied life. It flowed from her like light from a beacon. Whether nervous, as she'd been moments before, or still, as she was now, her entire being seemed to thrum with energy and passion. If he closed his eyes and concentrated on her, he could probably hear her heart beating in her chest, her silken, vibrant hair rustling against her elegant dress.

She was not at all as he'd expected her to be. Her demand of the Council had been childishly whiny, as if she'd been much younger than the sister, Charlene. And her threat to expose the Society was worse than ludicrous, it was damning. For her. If a diary existed, she should have burned it and scattered the ashes.

Yet she wore her vibrancy like a shield, and was as unlike her unfortunate sister as the twilight from the dawn. Of course, he'd only seen her sister once, when all the life had been drained from her.

Gavin had accomplished his mission then, a rescue of sorts. He'd dragged a maddened Jonathan from the room. Sickened by what his friend had been trying to do, attempting to make the Exchange with a woman already gone, he had consigned him to a fate worse than death among his kind. Jonathan had been banished, cast into utter isolation from the Society.

But now Gavin wondered about the events that led to that banishment, questioning what had really happened that terrible night. And staring at Tara Michaels, he puzzled over the magical allure these unusual sisters held for his kind.

He knew better than to look at her, for to meet her eyes was to feel a peculiar longing, not the furious drive he normally knew, the frantic pounding need that only a mortal could satisfy. The ache he felt for this woman was different. A hunger that didn't demand but rather enticed, a thirst that lured rather than insisted. If he looked at her, he knew he would experience a desire to slip into her arms, to crush her to his chest and drown in her essence.

But he looked nonetheless.

He didn't listen to her words about her sister, only the cadence of her velvet voice. He didn't hear her sorrow, but caught every nuance of her anger and detected a yearning that fueled the blaze of hunger burning in him.

Why had she challenged the Council? If she'd left them alone, she would have been safe. As it was, she'd flung down the most dangerous of gauntlets—threatening to reveal their darkest secrets. And he'd been sent to put an end to her insolence—to crush her. But he would do so in his own time.

She paused in her speech and her eyes lifted to his. He met them steadily. And was washed with a craving for her so intense and so strong that he felt rocked by it. The woman had no inkling of the forces she'd challenged, he thought even as his lips curved into a smile.

And as she slightly returned his smile, he suddenly wanted to call out a warning to her. A warning no one had given him all those years ago.

Run, hide somewhere. She should change her name, her glorious hair. She should never go out at night, sleep all the remaining days of her mortal life in the safe bowels of a church, any church. Anything to mask her from the Council's wrath. From him.

Tara concluded her remarks and stepped down from the lectern. She touched people here and there, reaching a hand out to meet theirs, warm fingers brushing against shoulders or cheeks. And always she smiled softly, as if she possessed a secret that no one else in the room could possibly guess.

His whole body seemed to still as she neared his position. With one swift movement he could snatch her into his arms and whisk her from the room. No one present could stop him. Nothing could stop him except perhaps the concerted effort of the entire Council itself.

"Hello," she said softly. Then, startling him, she held

out her hand to him. He couldn't remember the last time a mortal had sought contact with him of her own accord.

Unlike his, her hand trembled a little. She looked up at him, though she was not much shorter than he. Her lips parted just enough to reveal her even teeth, her cheeks flushed, her eyes were luminous and revealed her mortality in the reflection of her unsullied soul. And yet she didn't appear frightened of him. That, too, was different.

By contrast, he was afraid as he hadn't been afraid for generations. And as he took her hand in his, enfolding it to his palm, he knew why he was frightened. He'd believed nothing could stop him from taking her if he chose. Now he suspected differently. *She* could stop him. Not with puny weapons of myth and vanity, crosses or vials of holy water, but with her sheer vibrancy and vitality.

"Tara Michaels," she said.

"I know," he answered and he felt a tremor run through her as he spoke. He drew her hand to the place where she could feel his heart beating. For his heart did beat, even after all these long years. Not as hers did perhaps, but with a steady and cold rhythm. Her fingers fluttered against his chest, fire against ice.

"I want…to thank you for coming," she said.

"That's one thing you shouldn't do," he said.

Her eyes widened and he saw a flicker of flame dance in them before it was doused by a fear. Her fingers quaked in his hand as if trapped there, though she could easily have pulled them away. Too easily.

She swallowed and straightened slightly, but she didn't remove her eyes from his. But he could feel her tension. He watched as she struggled for a decision. As if he could read her mind, he knew she didn't know whether to attempt dissimulation or to confront him boldly.

He was strangely proud of her when she chose a direct approach. "And you're Gavin Deveroux," she said.

"I am."

"My sister mentioned you in her diary," she said.

He raised an eyebrow, truly surprised at this revelation. Why would her sister have mentioned him? Perhaps the Council did have cause for some alarm. Jonathan must have told the sister much more than he ever should have if he'd bandied about Council members' names.

"That's why you're here," she said. "For the diary."

He acknowledged this with a single nod, though she'd only guessed a small portion of why he was there.

"You'll have to wait until the guests leave," she said. "I don't have it with me. I'm a lot like my sister, Mr. Deveroux, but then, she might have told you that."

"I didn't know your sister," he said.

Her eyes narrowed a little and he could see she disbelieved him. "You never knew Charlene…?" she prompted, as if giving him a second chance at acknowledging a truth that didn't exist.

"I only saw her the one time, and that under unpleasant circumstances," he said.

Now her disbelief was tinged with a hint of disgust. He frowned a little at her reaction. Why should she be so certain he lied?

"Only the once?" she said, like a prosecutor offering a witness on the stand an opportunity to change his testimony before he tangled himself inextricably in a web of lies.

"The night she died," he said.

If possible her eyes widened even farther. He realized she hadn't expected honesty from him even as she'd let it be clear she didn't believe him.

Considering her challenge, her confusion was baffling in

itself. She claimed, through the diary, to know all about his kind. Then she should know his kind never lied. There was no need for lies in the Society. Only mortals lied, as if in need to stave off the finality of death.

But Jonathan had lied, hadn't he, before his banishment?

"I don't know what to say," she said. And he thought it was true.

Her hand lay quiescent beneath his now. He could see the rapid beating of her pulse just above her finely shaped collarbone. He fought the urge to press his lips against her soft skin, to feel the vein beating there.

As if aware of his thoughts, her chin squared and her lids lowered slightly. Menacingly. He almost smiled at the notion of a mortal threatening him, however obliquely.

"I don't know much of what happened that night. Why don't you tell me what really happened," she said.

That was something he couldn't do. That night, a year before, he'd been sent to find Jonathan, to stop him from making a dreadful mistake, and instead had found a greater problem than the Council had dared even consider.

"I don't know much," he said.

"Really."

He smiled a little at that, rather enjoying the coldness of her words, the flat-voiced disbelief in her single word. Perhaps she was a woman who challenged anything and everything. She was certainly challenging him now. She'd discover her mistake all too soon. He wondered if she had any idea just how much danger she was in because of her challenges.

She drew a deep breath and glanced over her shoulder at the man she'd been standing with earlier. A man Gavin had seen before—the same night Jonathan had gone nearly insane and Tara's sister had perished. The man nodded at

Tara, a lowering of his head that he turned into a cough as he looked away trying to pretend no communication had taken place. More lies.

"Would you please tell me what you *do* know of that night?" she asked, making the request seem a purely socially correct response to his statement. "When everyone's gone, I mean."

"Yes," he said simply. He raised her hand to his lips and pressed a kiss against the back of her fingers.

A flicker of something he couldn't identify crossed her features, something akin to pain.

"I'm afraid…" she said, as if prepared to continued. But her words hung in the air between them, a declaration of fact, not a prelude to whatever it was she feared.

You should be, he thought. You signed your death warrant by your hints at blackmail. And your executioner holds your hand in his now. But confounding him almost as much as it startled her, he found himself saying, "Don't be frightened. I'll be here."

He released her then, letting her move away, needing to have her as far away from him as possible. He frowned heavily, trying to fathom why he'd spoken as he had. Was some unsuspected tender part of him trying to comfort her, lull her into trusting him so that the end, when it inevitably came, would be less painful for her? But his kind didn't hold tenderness in their limited repertoire of emotions.

People in the crowd claimed her, touching her, petting her. However, her laugh, when she released it, was now forced and shallow, as empty as any one of his kind. He physically ached to hear its simplicity again, and a thousand possible ways of drawing it forth played through his mind.

"Did you know Charlene well?" a voice at his shoulder asked.

He turned slightly, looking down into the gaze of a young woman with dye-blackened hair and bloodred lips outlined in black pencil. "No," he said shortly.

"I worked with her," the woman said. She licked her lips provocatively.

He deliberately shifted his gaze from the young woman who liked playing with fire to Tara, who looked as if she'd never even seen fire, let alone enjoyed playing with it. Of the two women, he instinctively understood that Tara was the stronger, that she needed no masks to reveal her inner self.

"That man over there...the one talking with Charlene's sister?...he was really torn up when she died. They were engaged. To hear Tom tell it, they were still engaged when she was killed, but I know that's not true. She was seeing someone else. They arrested him for her murder, you know. Not the other guy, they never found him, but Tom. What did you say your name was?"

"I didn't," he said, looking back down at her.

"Oh, goody," she said. The word sounded incongruous, coming from her overripe lips. "A guessing game."

Gavin watched as Tom took Tara's arm and pulled her away from the thinning crowd and whispered something to her. Every muscle in the man's body was tense with unspoken urgency. He made a curious hand gesture, pulling at the air with his fist before dropping his hand again and leaning into her. Tara turned her head away from the man. And she raised her eyes to meet his own, fear and some other emotion warring on her lovely face.

"Now, it can't be anything common. Not George. Hmm, not Sam or Bill. Something exotic, I think. Jeremy? Jason? How about Justin?"

"Do you know how Charlene died?" he asked, keeping his gaze on Tara.

"I heard she'd been beaten to death," the young woman answered, lowering her voice, but not enough to hide the note of excitement.

"She was. And her throat was ripped out."

"Oooh…no one ever told me. It wasn't in the papers. How do you know so much about it?"

Gavin glanced down at her. "I was there."

"You w-were th-there? I—I don't understand."

"No," he said. "You don't."

"Gavin?"

He turned to see Tara beside him. Her face was set and her eyes blazed slightly. In warning. *Leave her alone.* If she'd shouted the words aloud, he'd have heard them no less clearly. He smiled slightly. She was a fighter, this Tara Michaels. But a fighter like a small feisty child trying to fell its father with little flailing fists.

"Tara?" He mimicked her exact tone.

She looked at the young woman. "I don't mean to be rude, Helen, but I really have to talk to Mr. Deveroux alone for a moment."

Gavin watched as Helen hesitated, as if she wanted to argue, but the expression on Tara's face brooked no denial. Finally, after an incoherent murmur and a sideways glance at him, the young, too-heavily-painted woman moved away.

Trying to sort out Tara's almost fierce protectiveness of the foolish young woman, sifting through the possible reasons for her challenge to the Council, he felt a sudden sharp doubt. Her challenge hadn't said what she would do with the information she had in her possession. There had been no explicit threat.

What if the Council had made a mistake? What if it wasn't a challenge at all, but just an attempt to hand over the damning information written down in her sister's diary? He had to see the diary.

Not that it would make any difference. Once an edict was handed down, the Council never looked back and reflected on the wisdom of their decision. She was to be eliminated. Right or wrong, they expected their orders to be carried out.

What was troubling him? How could he doubt the Council? What was it about this woman that shook him so?

"Why did you send that girl away?" he asked. And the fact that he felt genuine curiosity was something else new to him.

She flicked him a cold glance, a knowing glance, and he found he didn't care for it. He preferred her smile, uncertain though it was. Something of this must have shown in his expression, for hers immediately shifted and she smiled a little, stepping a little closer to him.

"Jealousy?" she asked lightly, as though she thought he would accept that as her reason for chasing the woman away.

More lies, he thought, though at that moment he wished it was the truth. For jealousy, by its very nature, implied strong feelings. And he wanted her to feel as strangely and inexplicably drawn to him as he was to her.

"Are you saying you want me?" he asked bluntly.

"Yes," she said, and he could tell by the widening of her eyes, by the rapid rise and fall of her breasts beneath her dress that she wasn't lying now, though she was undoubtedly playing some game. She *did* want him.

But not nearly as much as he wanted her.

And as abruptly and surely as if he'd thought about it

for months and years, he understood that he wasn't going to accede to the Council's dictates on this occasion. Later perhaps, when he knew more. Or maybe when he regained his senses and grew tired of her. But for now, she would be his. And in all ways. And once she was his, as long as he remained a part of the Council, the other members could not touch her.

There was danger in taking this route. For her, certainly, but for him as well, and perhaps of the two, his would be the greater peril. For should he anger the Council, she would know a swift death, whereas he would be doubly cursed. Like Jonathan.

Even thinking this, he took her hand in his and drew it to his chest once more, pressing it to his heart. "Then be with me," he said.

"W-what?"

"Say yes," he murmured, too softly for anyone else to hear.

"I...I c—"

"Don't say you can't," he said. And suddenly her acceptance meant far more to him than he'd thought possible. He thought of the members of the Council. He thought of the shock that would ripple through the Society. He thought of Jonathan and his grief and rage. And he replayed this woman's laughter in his mind, felt the vibrancy that resonated through her and consequently through him.

What was he doing, what was he thinking? Would he defy the Council for this mortal woman? Could he? What then, give her a night or two to remember before snuffing that vitality from her?

Or would he grant her another fate, the one he'd intended for the reward he'd chosen, and turn her into a being like himself? Would he enact the ancient ceremony of the Exchange with this woman?

Either way, she would no longer be changed. The laughter he ached to possess from her would never sound again, for in his strange world she would never have cause for laughter. Death might have its humorous elements, but there was nothing remotely funny about living death.

"What are you asking me?" she asked, tossing her hair back now, a measure of haughtiness in her stance. Another challenge.

"To marry me," he said, shocking himself by the wild plan forming in his mind. It was a dangerous and potentially deadly scheme in direct defiance of the Council. What could he be considering? Going rogue, like Jonathan? No. He couldn't do that. And yet…perhaps there was a way.

"What?"

"Marry me," he said, suddenly forceful, drawing her a single step closer, never once letting her gaze falter from his. "Marry me, Tara Michaels. Now. Tonight."

Vaguely, as if from a thousand miles away, he heard his own words filter through his system. He was utterly damning himself. He would be ostracized, possibly killed for such a betrayal of orders. A rogue.

When something flickered in Tara's eyes, something oddly like triumph or perhaps extreme fear, he was brought back to his outrageous proposal to her. She was right to fear him. Fear would be her only hope of even living the life he led. Only the curse he lived under could allow her to draw breath once the Council discovered his motives for this unusual action.

Unless she *willingly* married him. Now. Tonight. Perhaps it would be marriage made in the darkest depths of hell, but it might spare her. Might. And heedless of his own danger, he wanted her spared. Because of her myriad challenges to his kind, or because she exuded such joy of life? Or because she drew him as none of her kind had ever done before?

"All right," she said, as if agreeing to take a cup of tea with him some afternoon.

He had no idea why she agreed. He could see some lingering triumph or terror in her gaze, but she didn't look away. He'd exerted no spell, woven no hypnotic magic upon her. She'd agreed of her own free will.

But a wild exultation raced through his veins, a heat he'd never known, even in his mortal life.

"This is Las Vegas. Almost every hotel in the city has a chapel," she said, as if calling his bluff.

"Bring the justice in here," he commanded, lest she change her mind. "These people can be witnesses."

Without taking her eyes from his, she lifted her free hand and called out for Tom. Within minutes he'd summoned a small man with a round face and a receding chin. Tara thought he eyed the couple incuriously before opening a book and asking their names.

She murmured hers and started a little when Gavin spoke his name in a strong tone.

Gavin asked, "It will be utterly binding?"

"Oh, yes," the small man said. "I'm a justice, legal and licensed. No church or judge could make you any more married than me."

"Good," Gavin said. "Let's do it then."

A shudder ran through this woman, who had agreed to be his bride. He wanted to follow the shudder with his hands, making her tremble for his touch, out of desire, not fear, or whatever motivated her now.

"You'll have to pay me now. You'd be surprised how

many couples get cold feet right after the 'I do' part. So if—''

"We understand," Gavin interrupted and produced his wallet.

As the little man accepted the crisp fifties, Gavin wondered if he was buying a marriage license, or a one-way ticket to disaster.

Chapter 3

Tara's hands shook as, less than an hour later, the creature named Gavin Deveroux slid a heavy and strangely warm signet ring from his hand and onto her finger. Dimly, she heard him promise to keep her in his heart for as long as they both lived.

She wanted to denounce him then, to cry out against this mockery of a wedding. For all that his heart had beat so steadily beneath her hand, she knew that he was not even alive, for God's sake. He was a man dwelling in a semi-dead state, cruelly draining the life from others...others like her sister Charlene, who had luckily been spared his curse thanks to Tom's last-second intervention.

And it was a very real possibility that her vow to live out her existence with him might not bind her longer than the next sunrise over the mountains that ringed Las Vegas. Mountains that would be visible from her motel-room window, only four floors above where they now stood. It was possible that she had less than eleven hours of married life to contemplate.

"Then I now pronounce you man and wife," Justice Olafsen intoned. Tara shook her head slightly. This wasn't even a *man* she'd married. Not in any classic definition of the term anyway. Though to look at him no one would ever guess that he was anything but pure human male, and more so than many.

She didn't dare look at him herself. Even as he held her hand tightly in his grasp she thought of the reasons why she'd agreed to marry him. Why he had wanted to marry *her* she could not guess, but it meant she could keep him in her room until the signal, and then Tom could finish what he'd vowed to do, on the night of Charlene's death; what he had plotted carefully during the months he'd spent in jail, when the police were convinced he had committed the murder. He could thank his lucky stars for DNA evidence. It was the only thing that had allowed him to go free.

And she would have her revenge and would have rid the world of a murderer that the law would never be able to touch. Why did the thought leave her feeling so empty, so lost?

"You may kiss your bride," the justice said, nodding to the quasi-immortal Tara had married.

Gavin—her *husband,* she thought wildly—pulled her hand to his chest yet again. She could feel his heart beating and again was surprised by it. She'd naively assumed that she would feel no such evidence of life.

For the third time that night, she was assailed by doubt. What if Tom was as crazy as she'd first thought, so many months before? What if the police, although they'd been forced to let him go once a jury of his peers had found him not guilty of the murder, had been right after all and there was no other murderer in the room that night?

What if she'd just married a totally innocent stranger, for no other reason than to lure him into a trap, and certain death? Was she the willing dupe in Tom's insanity and desire for revenge?

She met Gavin's eyes then, doubt warring with belief. She couldn't read what he was thinking, but the blaze in his eyes took her breath away. No, he knew who she was. He'd asked her about the diary. And while he hadn't admitted he'd known Charlene, he'd acknowledged that he'd been with her the night she was killed. Tom was right. She didn't dare doubt what she was doing. A creature like this had no right to be in the world, couldn't be allowed to remain in it.

"Tara," he said. "You are mine now."

She drew in her breath on a sharp, cold stab of fear. Tom *was* right. And, knowing that, believing that, she would play her part...take him to her room and use whatever power she had to hold him willing captive until dawn. And if she had to be his wife to be able to bind him until morning, then she would be his wife.

Gavin lowered his lips to hers and she was surprised a second time by his apparent humanity. His mouth, hot and fiery, covered hers, seized her breath. Shouldn't he be cold? Shouldn't she be repelled? But as his kiss captured her and his tongue sought the warmth of her mouth, she found herself leaning into his kiss, into his embrace.

And then she couldn't think of anything at all, she could only bask in his heat.

She felt more than saw the mourners, now wedding party, swarming around them, felt their hands on her back, on Gavin, and heard, as though from a great distance, a dull applause. These were Charlene's friends, not her own. They would be unaware Gavin was a complete stranger, just as they were unaware he wasn't human.

Gavin's lips were hot and silky and his tongue wove a magic she'd never known before. And as she instinctively returned his kiss, she realized the crowd wasn't clapping, it was her own heartbeat was hammering in her ears.

Ignoring the justice and witnesses, Gavin caressed her back, pulling her even more tightly to him, letting her know in no uncertain terms that he was humanlike in other ways as well. He hadn't lied when he said he wanted her.

Nor had she when she'd said she wanted him. It was wrong, it was crazy, but she did. God help her.

He abruptly released her mouth and dragged her against the thundering of his heart, pressing her face tightly against his silk shirt, his fingers entangled in her hair. She could hear him drawing ragged breaths and knew that on some level at least, he was as shaken by their kiss as she.

"Tara," he whispered. "Sweet Tara..."

She opened her eyes a little and saw Tom standing in the solarium doorway. His face was dark with black triumph and etched with a bitter loathing.

The rigid set of Tom's features reminded Tara that she'd just married her sister's murderer. The man who held her so closely to his broad chest, whose hand pressed so fiercely into her hair, who gasped for air like a drowning man, was a killer. Worse, he was a *vampire*.

She shuddered. Instead of releasing her, he lowered his velvet lips to her temple and pressed the gentlest of kisses there. She shivered at his touch, thinking of her sister's torn throat, trying not to lose that image.

When his lips lowered still further, nuzzling the highly sensitive hollow of her neck, she should have pulled back in horror, but instead found herself tilting to allow him greater access, encouraging this strange and mesmerizing creature to taste her, to kiss her as intimately as any husband might.

But he wasn't *any* husband…he was *hers*.

What in the name of heaven had she done?

As if he'd heard the question, he pulled back a little. Framing her face with his hands, his gaze was unwavering upon hers. His thumbs softly stroked the planes of her cheeks, slowly massaging her temples.

His touch lulled her, drugged her. And when his lips lowered to hers once again, she arched to meet his hard body, his hot kiss. Tom had to be wrong. This man wasn't ordinary by any means, but he couldn't be one of the living dead, he couldn't be a killer, a murderer. He was far, far too human. Nothing that felt this right could be so dreadfully wrong—could it?

Someone called out for champagne and someone else—Helen she thought—began singing some seventies love song in a clear and terribly off-key soprano. Somehow the pitch that should have been carried in a light and happy major key, slipped, in this woman's voice, to a discordant minor. And the dissonance seemed to underscore the iniquity of this marriage, the essential wickedness of it.

Gavin pulled back from her with a sigh that she took for reluctance, until she met his gaze once again. The expression on his face frightened her more than anything had since Charlene's death. Because he appeared more staggered by their union than she…and perhaps, even more afraid of it.

Why? What did he have to be afraid of? Charlene's diary? It was certainly incriminating enough…if anyone could ever be brought to believe what she had written. Certainly the police hadn't believed any of it. And the judge had dismissed it without a second reading.

She'd known her sister, probably known her better than anyone on the face of the earth—or had once—yet it had taken Tom months to convince her that her sister wasn't crazy, that she'd been hypnotized by a creature whose very nature was antithetical to humankind.

How could her sister have loved such a monster?

Gavin pulled her arm through the crook of his and ran his hand down the slope of her back, resting it lightly, surely at her waist.

And how could she, herself, have married him?

The loud popping of a champagne cork jolted through Tara as if she'd been shot. And she felt Gavin squeeze her hand a little too strongly, as if he too had been startled.

"A toast!" someone called out and the efficient hotel staff moved swiftly through the room, dispensing glasses of champagne.

"To the bride and groom," Helen said, after handing both Gavin and Tara a dripping glass. "May they find all the happiness they deserve."

And what exactly is it that we both deserve, Tara wondered. A murderer married to a would-be murderess. Dear God.

Tara's hand was shaking too much to lift the broad bowl of the glass to her lips. Champagne sloshed from the sides and spilled down her fingers and onto the floor. She watched it as if from a great distance, creating a superstition out of it, suddenly sure it must be bad luck for the bride to spill the wedding champagne.

She watched, almost dispassionately, as Gavin removed the glass from her hand and held it to her lips, tilting it to her as he raised his own glass to his mouth. She took a small sip at the same time he did, her eyes on his, strangely grateful for his help.

He handed their glasses away without looking to see who took them from him, then he used one finger to lift her still dripping hand to his lips. His tongue flicked out and caught a drop of champagne from first one finger then another, then slowly sliding each finger into his mouth to suckle away any residue of sparkling wine.

The crowd didn't fade away in her concentration of his tongue against her fingers, the people around them simply all fell silent in watching his blatant seduction of her senses. And someone gasped when all the golden liquid was gone and he turned her palm upward and drew it to his mouth and laved it with his tongue before closing his eyes as if in pain.

She realized it was she who had gasped, for her breath now released in staccato exhalations, almost whimpers of combined desire and fear.

He opened his eyes and a glint of something akin to mischief lit their fathomless depths.

Involuntarily, she chuckled.

As did he.

And she found herself laughing at the absurdity of her situation.

Which made him catch her to him and swing her up and into his arms. He cradled her against his chest, smiling down at her in as fierce a triumph as Tom had displayed earlier, but without a single shadow of bitterness staining it.

Someone tossed her slender handbag to her, someone else jumped for the doors and opened them with a flourish. Tom called out for her to "signal" him if she needed anything.

She said nothing as he strode through the doors and out into the broad, red-carpeted hallway leading to the glimmering brass elevators.

"It was your laugh, you know," he said, as he halted before the elevators.

"My laugh?"

"You have a room here in the hotel, don't you?" he asked, though it was more statement than question.

"Yes. Fifth floor."

The elevator doors opened. Without setting her down, he carried her across the threshold of the elevator and leaned to depress the proper button.

"My laugh?" she asked again, strangely relaxed in his arms, oddly reluctant to be set down and released.

"Tara's harp," he said, lowering his lips to hers, not letting her ask anything further.

But with his lips upon hers, she could think of nothing else anyway.

Chapter 4

The moment the stranger, who was now her husband, set her down in the room that was to be their wedding bower, Tara realized that she had not thought of what to do once she got Gavin Deveroux beyond her hotel room door. Looking back, she thought that she must have somehow believed that the hours until dawn would miraculously fly by. That she would open the bedroom curtains halfway then close them again, signaling Tom that his moment of glory was at hand.

Now, standing before the seemingly endless expanse of the king-sized bed, still trembling from the intensity of Gavin's kisses, she understood how foolish she and Tom had been. She most of all. Almost ten hours stretched before her until dawn. That could be a lifetime spent with this stranger. With a murderer.

With her husband on their wedding night.

Dry-mouthed, she averted her gaze from the too-large

bed and from the too-powerful man standing too close to it.

The plush hotel room had seemed enormous before, but now felt composed of nothing but pathways to a monstrous bed. A place she desperately wanted to go to with this stranger...and didn't dare to.

"Tara...?"

She couldn't look at him. Not with the thought of all those hours looming before them. And most of all, not with the clear understanding that he literally mesmerized her.

"Tara, we have to talk."

His words were so traditionally suited to a wedding night tête-à-tête that she involuntarily glanced up at him. She was stunned to find him looking uncomfortable and nervous, as if he were any normal groom who had to tell a new bride a sorry tale of his past. If he'd been wearing a collar, he would have been running his finger around it.

What was he going to tell her? Honey, there's something I forgot to tell you before we got married...I really hate garlic...oh, and I'm not keen on picket fences either.

She couldn't help it, she began to giggle and then to laugh in earnest, though her laughter carried a note of hysteria obvious even to herself. It halted as abruptly as it began when he shifted as if to move toward her.

Where she'd leaned into his kiss only moments earlier, she now took a step back and felt the edge of the bed press against her knees. She half expected anger or even his commanding presence to leap into action, but instead she saw a flash of what, in anyone else, she would call plain and simple hurt.

Gavin halted in midstride, trying to understand the strange sensation roiling in his chest. It wasn't hunger, or desire. It was something half familiar, and painful, as if someone had wrapped a huge fist around his heart and squeezed it.

He'd experienced many a mortal stepping away from him in fear. That was part of the chase, part of the taking. The ill, the infirm, those who sought the path of danger…those were the Society's preserve. But Tara's shrinking back from him was different somehow, unexpected. And the pain that single step caused him, the sensation inside him, was new…and yet not. He almost recognized it.

If she were any other woman, if she were not his wife by his own willing vow, he would move more swiftly than any mortal could and seize her to him, drawing from her anything he pleased. But however strangely it had come about, Tara *was* his wife. As willingly his as he was her husband.

For the first time since his Crossing to the Society, he wondered what it would feel like to be a mortal again. Just a man. Vulnerable and defenseless. A man who could inspire love and tenderness. A man who could weave a spell of his own simply by experiencing emotions to their fullest extent.

And he wondered if it would be possible to have a woman come to him of her own volition, not under the compulsion of the spell he would weave over her, before robbing her of some measure of life's essence.

He took another step toward her, telling himself that this woman had willingly married him, had leaned into his kisses, clung to his lips as if drugged by them.

He stopped, remembering the conversation he'd witnessed between her and Tom, the mortal he'd seen at the scene of her sister's death. Remembered the look of hatred on the man's face.

Tara had married him with an ulterior motive. But her kiss hadn't lied. Was there a difference between response and coming to him freely? Suddenly he wanted to know. Craved the knowledge.

"Tara…" he said slowly. And, just as slowly, she raised her eyes to meet his. A moment ago she'd been laughing, not the same laugh as before, but over something that had both amused and frightened her. Now she was almost utterly still.

"You know what I am," he said.

As if she were a puppet and he the master, she nodded jerkily. He felt more than saw the fear in her eyes.

"Why did you marry me?" he asked, desperate to understand her, as if it might explain his own actions on this bizarre night.

She opened her mouth to reply, then shut it again. She shook her head, not as if she didn't know the answer but, he thought sadly, as if the telling would cause her pain. Or was it him she was trying to spare? The notion caused his breath to catch for a moment and a thousand possible explanations to spin in his mind.

"Can you show me the diary?" He was strangely reluctant to even mention it, but desperate to see it. He had to know if she'd unwittingly challenged the Council, hadn't deliberately threatened his kind's existence. What if she'd just been trying to warn them? Simple ignorance had to be the reason she'd foolishly placed her life in such danger.

Her eyes widened. "I-it's not here," she said.

He shook his head. "You can't lie to me, Tara. Any more than I can lie to you. Surely your sister mentioned that, somewhere in her diary. Surely she knew our kind have no need for lies."

Again he thought of Jonathan, how he'd lied about his

liaison with Charlene. How he'd cried when he'd been unable to complete the action that would have ensured her Crossing.

He took another step toward her, not really caring now if she tried to evade him or not.

But she didn't move away from him, though she stiffened. She lifted her chin and met his gaze in a combination of defiance and assessment. Nothing could have stopped him more effectively, though he wasn't certain why. It was as if she held her mortality out as protection. Her sheer vulnerability made him halt.

He ran a hand through his hair, pulling it back from his face, much as he wanted to sweep hers from her brow. He held his breath as her eyes traveled the line of his forearm to his biceps and his shoulders. He felt as if she kissed him when her gaze lifted to his lips, and touched him when they fell to his chest. He slowly lowered his arms and rested his hands on his upper thighs and felt a sharp knifepoint of triumph when her eyes flicked from his hands to the apex of his thighs, widened for a moment, then darted back up again.

The stain of red that flushed her cheeks warmed him more than any fire ever had. No, her kisses had not lied.

"What did you mean when you said, 'Tara's harp'?" she asked softly, her eyes on his now, her lips soft and moist. "When we were in the elevator?"

"It's from an old poem," he said, equally softly, suddenly aware how the stanza ended, not wanting her to know its conclusion. Unwilling to let her understand that her undoing would most certainly come at his hands.

She frowned, and he smiled, for he could tell she was sifting through all the poetry she knew and was still drawing a blank. He felt another frisson of familiarity, a rather banal enjoyment of something as uncomplicated as teasing this mortal beauty with a curious line of poetry.

"Thomas Moore," he prompted, consciously editing the lines, choosing a different emphasis to avoid telling her the finale.

Her frown deepened, but her eyes lit and a slight smile tugged at her lips. She shook her head finally and shrugged, lifting her hands as if in defeat.

She'd never know what effort it took not to claim those delicate fingers and draw her to him.

The harp that once through Tara's halls
The soul of music shed...

Had he been a mortal man only, he might have missed the softening of her features, the sudden relaxation of her shoulders. As it was, he saw every ripple of her reaction to his words and knew that she'd understood his reference with lightning-quick brilliance. She accepted on multiple levels his likening of her laughter to a harp that shed the soul of music itself. A shimmer of tears glistened in her beautiful eyes.

He could not remain where he was and not touch her. He could not resist the soft allure of her face, any more than he could have walked into a church or willingly thrown himself onto a wooden stake.

"Tara..." he breathed, making a vow of her name.

And, as if answering every wish he'd ever had, she stepped toward him, and slid into his embrace like a mermaid into water, fluid and graceful. He shuddered at her soft touch and enfolded her to him gently. Reverently. Almost fearfully. But with a true and aching desire to hold her close, to drown in this want for her.

"Tara," he whispered.

"Gavin," she murmured back.

Somewhere deep inside him, he felt the link, the connection that bound them, a tie far deeper than penning their names on a sheet of paper signed by a justice. And he shuddered with the realization of how strongly he ached for her.

Ah, Jonathan, he thought, *I didn't know. None of us knew.* He reveled in the feel of Tara's pliant, silken body in his arms, and a glimmer of understanding struck him; now he knew why such tender contact with a mortal was forbidden by the Council. Taking, seizing, those were acceptable, but feeling this odd desire to cherish, that was the greatest crime of all. Because to do that was to render the whole Society in jeopardy.

And for the first time since his Crossing he understood why, because those feelings made him long to lay his whole sordid past at her feet, to tell her every dark secret in his soul. For absolution perhaps? For acceptance? He didn't know. He only knew the urge to reveal everything to her raged in him like a hurricane.

He could feel her heart beating against him. He could feel the soft weight of her breasts pressing to his chest. He heard the whisper of her dress moving against his shirt, the material so thin the two of them might as well have been naked.

And she was his *wife*. Achingly slowly, he approached her, his body at war with his mind, his need battling his newfound desire to keep her safe from harm, safe from *him* and all his kind.

How many years had it been since desire had been a pure thing for him? How many lifetimes had passed since he'd known even a measure of the sweetness of a single, lingering kiss?

With a low growl of pain and acceptance, he tasted her and knew he was lost.

There in her arms, feeling her timid caresses, he was a doomed being. He was an immortal trapped forever in a half existence now, craving that which he could never fully have, because love was alien to his kind.

But he wanted it, deserved or otherwise. He wanted Tara to love him. Just love him.

Tara didn't understand why she'd moved into his arms. She wondered if anyone really knew the reasons why they craved a certain touch, ached for the feel of a pair of lips pressed to their own. She knew it wasn't love, but it wasn't mere passion either. Something indefinable, some magic wove a spell between them and drew them together.

She could tell in the gentle stroking of his hands, in the trembling she felt in his fingers, the shuddering of his body that he was as moved by their touching as she was. And on some level he was as vulnerable to her as she was to him, perhaps even more so, though the concept was inexplicable.

She tried telling herself that she trembled out of fear of him, but she knew that was a lie. He'd said she couldn't lie to him, and it seemed he was right; she couldn't even lie to herself. She didn't just want this man—this being— she was stirred by him. Perhaps by the vulnerability she felt in his touch, the look of sorrow and pain in his eyes. And by his strange honesty.

If she could believe his words, then could she believe his lips, the graze of his fingers across her back, her jawline, the swell of her breasts?

"Ah, Tara...I've never wanted anyone in the way I want you," he murmured, his hot breath tickling her ear.

Neither had she, she thought, raising her hand to thread her fingers into his mane of hair. He moaned softly and moved his lips to her mouth, framing her face with his warm hands, deepening his kiss, deepening her longing for him.

She felt him shaking against her, knew his desire for her was as intense as hers for him. And she suspected that a battle raged in him, every bit as strong as the confusion that roiled in her. She could feel it in the difference in his kisses, in the tenderness and reverence his touch now displayed.

And he confirmed it when he drew back slightly and lifted his head. His eyes, heavy-lidded and glazed with desire, met hers steadily and yet with an odd plea in them. "I vow this, Tara Michaels, I will never willingly harm you."

She thought about his words, the sincerity of them, but the warning also. Never *willingly* harm her. Unwillingly he was capable of anything. And she realized that she could set aside her fear of what this might mean, that her trusting body was far more in charge of her mind than her fearful heart.

"I'm not Tara Michaels," she murmured.

He frowned at her and his head tilted sideways a little, considering her statement.

She smiled a little. "I'm Tara Deveroux now, remember?"

She didn't know why the simple teasing question would spark a sudden conflagration in him, but when he caught her to him for a fierce, demanding kiss, she half chuckled, infused with that sense of power that only such responsiveness could bring. As she returned his kiss, she had a strange feeling that the Fates, whoever and wherever they were, had just linked arms in harmony.

And when he pressed her back onto the large bed, she didn't resist. Nor did she evade his hands roaming her dress, molding it to her, exploring her through the gossamer material.

She tried telling herself that she allowed his caresses because she'd vowed to keep him in her room until dawn, by any means she could. But when he parted her dress, pressing his lips to the bared skin above her lacy bra, she couldn't pretend she was there for any reason but her own desire.

"Tara..." he murmured, his long, slender fingers gently peeling back her dress, his knuckles grazing the rise of her breasts. "You are so beautiful. You are like life itself, mysterious, incredible, frightening."

She thought that he might have been unaware he'd even spoken aloud, that he was voicing some philosophy from deep within him, for she could hear the note of wonder and sorrow in his tone.

While she didn't understand him at all, with his hands upon her, his touch sure and powerful yet achingly reverent, the importance of dawn seemed to slip away as easily as her clothing.

And as his lips nuzzled a nipple he'd bared to his view, she stopped trying to find rationalizations, reasons why her fingers threaded into his hair, explanations for why her body arched to meet his or why a throaty groan rose in her throat. She could only feel.

And however wrong it might be, the very devil's touch felt so very right.

Chapter 5

Gavin had believed he knew all there was to know about magic, about spells cast on dark nights. In the years since the Crossing, he'd known every physical pleasure, every nuance of lust. And nothing he'd ever encountered had prepared him for Tara.

Somehow she wove a magic far greater than any allure he could ever have conjured. And it was pure, raw magic, for it was born of her life essence. This magnificent woman straining up to meet his hand, moaning beneath his kisses, was truly and wholly *there* with him. Every motion, each slight brush of his lips upon her dewy skin sparked a response in her, not merely a physical one, but one born of deep, empathetic emotion.

It made him feel powerful on a level he'd never experienced before. And in that power was a responsibility, a trust. He ached to fulfill her every wish, to make this one night a memory to withstand all time. For it could well be their first and their very last.

He rested on his knees above her, running his hands down her glorious length, exploring every curve, contouring each and every rise and fall of her. And when she reached a hand to touch him, he gently pushed her fingers away, unwilling to be distracted by her questing.

He knew she still had to fear him on some level, knowing what he was, unwilling or unable to comprehend the half of his true nature. But he was utterly and profoundly humbled by the fact that she opened herself to him as the night opened to the gentle probing rays of the moon.

He, who lived in a dark world, made no move to douse the lights. He needed to see her, to watch her half-closed eyes, to watch her parted lips abruptly close and clench only to open again on a gasp as his fingers danced on the smoothness of her skin.

She reached for the tails of his shirt and tugged the silky material up and over his shoulders, and chuckled a little when it tangled in his hair.

He'd forgotten that laughter and joy could play a part in lovemaking. And as he felt her laughter eddy through him, within the depths of the soul he'd long abandoned, he realized joy *should* play all parts, be present in every kiss, each exploratory touch.

How long had it been since a woman had sighed at the feel of his skin beneath her fingers? How long had it been since he'd reacted to a touch with other than primal response? Years? A century? More?

All he knew was that he *never* wanted to forget what he was now feeling, never wanted to go back to the emptiness he'd known for so very long.

But how could he keep these fragile new feelings alive? How could he keep them safe, however uncomfortable they were? He would be gone by dawn, leaving her alone until the sun set again. He would have to go, because his kind could never stay with a mortal after the sun began its rising.

He stilled his touch on her full breast. By an inadvertent course, he'd arrived at the very reason the Society forbade *love* with a mortal. His kind were at their most vulnerable in the daylight hours, not wholly stripped of their powers, but almost as vulnerable as a mortal. And *love* would surely make one want to share that vulnerability.

"Gavin...?"

He stared down at her, certain suddenly that the reason she'd married him was to trap him until dawn, until he was at his most vulnerable. The realization should have saddened him, he thought, or angered him. Strangely, however, it only made him sad for her. Because he knew instinctively that she was as torn as he was.

What an unholy union they had forged between them, he thought. Both of them set to harm the other and yet both too strongly drawn to do anything other than sink into the glorious warm waters of...of what? It certainly couldn't be love. He was incapable of those emotions. So what mysterious, elusive emotion was it?

As if reading his mind, and understanding his confusion, she raised her hands to his face. And, as he'd done to her earlier, she drew her fingers over his eyes, closing them, and molded the shape of his face in her palms.

"Ahh, Gavin," she murmured, "I don't understand what's happening here...and I'm not sure I care to."

She lowered her hands to his shoulders and gently pushed him from his position above her. He didn't resist, but rolled on his back, a thousand disconnected thoughts firing through his mind, through his body. When she rolled over him, a shy smile on her lips, a question he couldn't understand in her eyes, he answered the only way he knew how…with a kiss.

And she returned the kiss with hungry passion, but with a touch of playfulness as well, running her slender fingers down the muscled planes of his chest, the tapered indentation of his waist and lower, to tickle at his trousers.

As aroused as he was by her touch, he was far more aroused by her unabashed want of him. With Tara, for the first time, it was a reciprocal desire. She was seducing him every bit as much as he was her, maybe more.

He decided that if he perished in that moment and could carry the memory of her lips upon him, he would die happily. But he couldn't die, not then, not now. And, for the first time in what seemed forever, he wanted to live. Really live. If nothing else, but for this moment, this time with Tara.

In all her life, Tara had never known such a freedom as she felt with this man, this creature who was now her husband. It couldn't be simply because of the weight of his ring on her finger, and it probably had less than nothing to do with his being a stranger both to her and to her kind. She was certain it wasn't an element of danger, fear inspiring lust. It was far more than any of those things.

As she bent to his chest and lightly flicked his hard nub of a nipple and he moaned in response, she felt centered somehow, as if everything she'd ever done or said in her entire lifetime had led her to this single moment.

Perhaps it had something to do with his saying he would know if she lied and that his kind could never lie. Maybe that concept created a cushion for their joining, a safety net that she'd never felt before.

Then as she met his eyes, she saw that sorrow she'd glimpsed earlier. She stilled her hands. "Gavin...?"

She felt his muscles contract beneath her fingers, as if he were holding himself ready for some blow. "Why do you look so sad sometimes?" And even as she asked the question, she was struck by her use of the word "sometimes," as if she'd known him for more than the few hours that night.

The room was so quiet that she heard the outside street noises, dim and soft. And she heard his breathing, slowing now and steadying.

"Because you make me want things I shouldn't want," he said finally.

"Things like this?" she asked and elaborated by running a hand down his side.

She heard his swift intake of air. "That, yes. And much more."

"Such as?" she asked, needing to know. Aching to know.

He turned his head away, as if ashamed of his feelings or thoughts. Or perhaps as confused as she felt. His eyes closed. A muscle in his jaw flexed and stilled. She thought that, whatever sorrow had seized him, he still appeared far more human than any man she knew.

She stretched a hand to his chin and gently pulled him back to face her. "Such as...?" she repeated, almost hating herself for needing to ask, sorry to see his eyes shadowed again, darkened with the pain she felt emanating from him.

He could have resisted her soft demand, but didn't. He allowed himself to be propelled toward her and opened his remarkable hazel-gold eyes.

He seemed to study her forever before answering. "You make me want things that mortals want. Things like your laughter, your touch. Yes, and more. Things like dreaming, wishing. Hoping. Things I don't know how to do, Tara. Things I've forgotten. You make me want them.''

"And is that so bad?'' she asked, as though not thoroughly staggered by his revelation. He'd no idea how much his straightforward answer rocked her.

He closed his eyes again, as if in pain. "You'll never know,'' he said. "I hope to God you never find out.''

His eyes opened and he lifted his hand to gently trace one of her breasts. She didn't break their locked gazes. His fingers slowly, carefully enclosed her nipple and rolled it between them.

"Ahh,'' she sighed and closed her own eyes then, letting the sensation of his touch wash over her, stealing all thought.

She turned her face to his caress and gently snared one of his fingers, much as he'd done earlier to her when he'd kissed the champagne from her hands. She heard his sharp intake of air as she pulled his finger into her mouth with tongue and lips and closed her eyes as she drew upon it.

He gave a low soft moan that almost seemed more a growl, and raised his free hand to her breast to mold her to his palm, to lift as if testing the weight of it, and then to rise slightly and capture her hard nipple between his knowing lips.

This time it was Tara who moaned, leaning in to this being who was no man, but whose ring she wore on her finger. And as she rocked forward, he raised his lips to hers and captured her, and the last moment when it might have been possible for her to withdraw, to pull away from him once and for all, fled and disappeared into the night.

He'd likened her laughter to a harp, now some hitherto untouched part of her soul melted at his caresses, and she raised her head to quote poetry to him, a snippet from some Longfellow poem she'd learned in college. He stilled as she spoke, his hands spanning the dip of her back, holding her tightly to his heated body.

"How you make me feel, Gavin."

He shifted her a little, moving a hand to the hollow between her breasts and pressing it to her chest.

She laid her own hand over his and felt its steady rhythm. "Yours still beats," she said softly, perhaps questioningly.

He gave the merest ghost of a chuckle. "I should say, 'For you.'"

"But you can't lie to me," she murmured, half smiling, half sad, wishing that he could.

"I think, just now…it wouldn't be a lie, Tara."

Suddenly she couldn't lie to him either, by word or by omission. She tried to get up, to pull out of his arms, but he held her fast against him, his hand still wedged between her breasts, and behind her, a single hand only, but holding as firmly as a band of steel.

"Gavin…"

"Let me kiss you, Tara."

"Gavin, I really have to—"

"Let me taste you."

"You don't understand. There's something—"

"There's always going to be *something,* Tara. For now, let's forget the universe. Just you and I. Together. Husband and wife."

His hand between her breasts shifted and slowly, gently contoured her rounded globes. "Gavin…"

"Let me at least pretend this is done in love. Surely we can give ourselves that, try to convince each other that I love you and you love me in return. Let me feel all that a mortal feels, let me drown in this fantasy. Tara, let me drown in you.''

Strangely, he'd said all this without undue passion in his voice, without pressure from his hands or even a quickening of his heartbeat, and yet Tara felt his longing rage through her like an unchecked fire.

And she slid without resistance into his kiss, fitting her hands to his bare torso, clinging to the hard muscles that rippled beneath her touch, willing to pretend with him.

Suddenly she was all too aware that there was less pretense than reality in her kisses.

Chapter 6

Gavin knew that he was doomed. In his plea for her, in her soft acceptance of his fabrication of love, he'd crossed the barrier between truth and fantasy. And the truth was, he wanted her as he'd never wanted anyone before. And the more damning truth was that he didn't know what love was, and couldn't begin to understand how he really felt about this glorious woman in his arms.

But with her, he came closer to a glimmer of understanding than he would ever have dreamed possible. And it made him want her all the more because of it. Not just for one night, but for tomorrow night, and all the tomorrow nights after.

Her hair brushed against his shoulders as her teeth lightly nipped at his chest, causing shudders of pleasure to dance through him. He rolled her over and imitated her actions and felt like laughing aloud in triumph when she gasped and arched to meet his lips.

He ran his hands down her lush curves, pulling her up to meet him. His senses reeled at the delicate texture of her skin, the way her breath caught slightly in ragged longing.

She wrapped her arms around him, drawing him closer to her, washing his dark thoughts away with her kisses. He longed to bury himself within her, to stay with her forever. A daylight longing, not one born of the night.

When she reached for his belt this time, he didn't argue or try to restrain her. Everything in him ached to join her, not to take her, but to give to her, to fill her with his need.

After she pushed his pants down his long legs, he brought his mouth down to her full breasts, kissing first one then the other. Then, as her body writhed beneath him, he moved still lower.

He closed his eyes and inhaled slowly, drinking in her scent, needing to be closer, aching to taste her. She tried pulling away as he spread her open to his view, to his touch, but he held her there, asking her to stay with him.

As if in answer, she relaxed on the bed, her thighs parting for him. He lowered his mouth to her, tasting her, slowly, gently laving her as his fingers slid into her. He knew he would never be the same again. Knowing that she was thoroughly open to him, despite his nature, in spite of her fears, changed him. Somehow her very acceptance of him at that moment granted him a measure of absolution.

Years and years of darkness melted away and he was a man again, a mortal, and terribly afraid of losing something precious. And when she pleaded with him to stop, to join her, it took every ounce of strength he had to stay where he was.

"Oh, Gavin, please..."

Never had she felt so utterly free. All thoughts of right and wrong, of should or shouldn't, were as distant to her as the morning, and as meaningless. Only Gavin himself and what he was doing to her had any impact on her consciousness.

Suddenly, he stilled.

Her entire body quivered for him, poised and aching for him to continue. She called his name and was surprised to only hear a whimper. Then cried his name in earnest as he resumed his onslaught. She knew she was lost. Hurled into the unknown, she sobbed out for him, needing to be caught, to be brought back to the earth. Over and over again she called his name as she spun about in the storm, shaking.

Finally, he raised his head to kiss her thigh, trailing his lips up the curve of her hip, and slowly withdrew his fingers.

"Gavin?" she asked, able to focus on him again.

His own gaze was glassy, his need etched on every plane of his beautiful face.

She held out her arms and he slid into them as if coming home, as though he'd embraced her just so a million times before. His long hair brushed against her face, and then spilled onto her shoulders. As she felt him at her entrance, she raised her hips to snare him.

She knew he would have moved slowly, gently, but gave him no option as she arched still further and encased him fully, pulling him down to sink into her as deeply as possible. His groan echoed her own softer sigh of relief.

He called her name as he settled against her. His eyes were closed and his head thrown back a little, a look of exquisite pleasure on his face.

As she wrapped her legs around his back, pressing him still more deeply within her, she felt his whole body shudder. He thrust his hands beneath her back and clung to her shoulders, pulling her down to meet his thrust.

Murmuring her name against the soft hollow of her throat, he slowly, achingly slowly, withdrew then entered again, teasing her, tormenting them both.

She found his hard buttocks and pulled him even tighter and harder against her. As if this were a signal to him to speed his thrusts, he began rocking into her with greater passion. She found herself arching to meet each thrust, her breath snared in her throat, her body thrumming to his every movement.

Murmuring her name, he drove into her with faster and faster strokes. Harder, deeper. Whispering her name, then calling it aloud with every thrust. "Tara…Tara…*Tara!*"

She felt that tingling, fading away sensation that presaged another leap into that wild storm, and clung to him, crying out his name, begging him to leap with her. And suddenly he went completely rigid, pulsating inside her, suddenly hot and quivering. He threw her from that cliff's edge a second time, but held her fast as he followed her over.

Tears of relief, spent passion, and a thousand different emotions slid from her eyes and trailed down her temples. As he slowly relaxed in her arms, he kissed the tears away. He did not ask why they were there, but accepted them for the release they were.

When he would have shifted to give her greater breathing room, she settled her arms around him, needing to feel his solid weight against her. She ached to feel his full body pressed against her. And was unwilling to let them part.

"I can't ever let you go, Tara," he said. "Wrong as it is, I won't be able to do it."

Lying within his warm embrace, Tara felt the magic begin to ebb away. Doubts, questions, even recriminations filled the void that magic left behind.

What had she done? How could she have succumbed to his allure? She couldn't kid herself that she'd done it to trap him. Nor could she pretend she'd done it for Charlene, or anyone on the face of the earth but herself.

She couldn't even lie to herself long enough to believe that he'd ensnared her with his sorrow. However inexplicable it was, she had joined him of her own accord. She was forced to acknowledge that she had never experienced anything remotely as wonderful before. And she knew, in some deep part of her heart, that she never would again without Gavin.

Tom had been desperately wrong about Gavin and his kind. He'd called them soulless devils. But this man holding her so tenderly had more heart and more soul than any man she'd ever known.

"Gavin...?" she asked, knowing she couldn't put off telling him about the morning any longer. Because she knew now that she would not be signaling Tom.

"Yes," he replied slowly, as if half aware of what she was about to say.

Haltingly at first, then gathering strength, she told him about Tom, about their plan to trap him and kill him when he was vulnerable. About all of it, except that she couldn't bring herself to talk about Charlene. Or Charlene's love of this creature, though she now understood her sister's feelings.

"Why are you telling me this now?" Gavin asked.

"Because I can't go through with it," she said simply.

His body jolted, then stilled as if he'd been hit. "Because of this?" he asked, holding her still closer. "What we shared?"

She gave a half shrug, not willing to reveal how very close she was to admitting that by some miracle—or curse—she was falling in love with him. With her sister's murderer. With a monster who wasn't even human.

He pressed a kiss to her temple and lingered there. Somehow she knew he had his eyes closed, that he was kissing her as if sealing some vow.

"Tara," he said, making her name part of that vow.

She said nothing, only waited.

"You didn't have to tell me anything."

Oh, but she had, though she wasn't certain of her reasons.

"And this was why you married me?"

She nodded, ashamed of it now.

"But that wasn't why you made love to me."

She shook her head.

"Why did you?"

Telling him she'd wanted to would have been the truth, but such a small element of the whole truth that she couldn't say the words. "Why did you want to marry me?" she countered.

She sensed some inner war raging in him. He moved against her as if to leave. She clung to his arms and held him there.

"To save you," he said finally.

"What?"

"Why did you challenge the Council?"

"I—Tom thought...the diary?"

At his nod, she said, "Just to bring you here."

"But if you didn't want anything from the Council—"

"We—Tom—wanted you."

"Why me in particular?"

"Because of Charlene."

"But I didn't even know Charlene. I only saw her the one time."

She stiffened in his arms. He'd said he couldn't lie to her. But perhaps that statement itself had been a lie. Suddenly her anger at his lie softened and ebbed. It was no use being angry at him, at a creature such as he. She'd gone to him willingly. A bride to her groom. But the realization did discolor the beautiful memory of what they'd shared.

She said sadly, "Charlene wrote about you in her diary."

"She wrote about me," he said, slowly. It was a statement, not a question.

"Yes. About how much she loved you. About your love for her."

"I see," he said. "And knowing this, you made love to me nonetheless."

"Yes," she replied simply, feeling tears gather in her eyes.

"And now you're willing to let me go, and not exact revenge."

"Y-yes," she said.

"Why, Tara?"

She shook her head, unable to answer him. A tear spilled free and fell onto his shoulder.

He raised his hand to touch his fingers to the tear, then to her face to capture another before it fell. "Tara... I don't know what your sister wrote in her diary, but it wasn't me she was with. I told you the truth, I didn't lie to you... I can't lie to you."

Her breath hitched on a sob. She wanted to believe him. Everything in her *ached* to believe him. But so much of what Charlene had written in the diary *was* the truth. Why would she lie about his name?

Gavin felt as if each tear that fell from her eyes seared his skin with its landing. He knew she didn't believe him, and wondered at the pain this knowledge brought him. He wanted her to believe. Wanted her to trust him, without ever having given her cause to do so.

But she had trusted him, with her body, with her heart that night. And even now with all her doubts, she still lay within his arms, not even asking for an explanation.

That much he could give her. She should know to her very soul that she'd not had a union with her sister's murderer.

He ran his fingers lightly over her face, wiping away her tears. Then he turned her so he could look down into her lovely eyes, so that she could read the truth in his.

"Jonathan was the one your sister loved, not me. He was exiled from the Society for loving her."

Her tears checked and her eyes searched his face for the truth. He saw a glimmer of hope cross her features. Then she frowned. "Exiled, why?"

"It's impossible for one of our kind to love one of yours."

Chapter 7

Tara's tears had subsided, but Gavin could still read confusion on her lovely face. "But—"

"Love, not take," he said, hoping he wouldn't have to elaborate.

She blinked as the understanding of his words sank in. And he saw another question form a frown on her brow.

He answered it before she could voice it. "I said it was impossible. I should have said it was forbidden."

"So it's not...impossible?"

He wondered if it was only his wishful thinking that detected a note of hope in her choked voice. Much as he would have liked to look away, his gaze remained fixed. "No, but in the history of the Society, it's only happened twice." Jonathan and one other.

He watched her assimilate this. "Twice. In how long?"

"Centuries, Tara. Millennia. Back to the beginning of man's history. And ours."

"You were a man once," she said. Her words hung between them like a sword. And he could tell they cut her every bit as much as they did him.

"Yes," he said. "I still am, Tara. But a man who is immortal."

"That's a contradiction," she said firmly. "An immortal being, by its very nature, can't be killed. A man can be."

"All things can be killed," he corrected. "Even seeming immortals. Just not by the same ways and means of a mortal man. Or woman."

"I don't understand."

"No. And it doesn't matter."

"This Jonathan…did he love my sister?"

"Yes. I truly think he did."

"Is he dead?"

"I don't know."

"Why did he kill her?"

Gavin shook his head. "I don't know what happened that night, Tara. Jonathan was insane by the time I arrived at the scene. He was like any human who lost a lover."

He wished he could bite the words back. This was her sister he was talking about. He'd had a sister once, so long ago now that he couldn't even recall the color of her eyes. But surely he'd cared about her.

Tara had cared enough for her sister to want to kill for her.

"But surely eventually someone asked him about what occurred between them."

"He was exiled before anyone asked," he told her, though he didn't add that no one had particularly cared what had happened that night. The only concern had been to secure Jonathan and save the Society. They were outside the rules and confines of mortal law. And they had their own stringent justice system.

"But surely just loving a woman couldn't be that much of a crime."

"It's dangerous. Not just to the immortal, but to the Society as a whole."

"Why?"

He wanted to shake her. Surely she of all people knew why. She herself had planned to trap him for the night and kill him with the dawn. Just as he'd planned to do with her. "To love is to be vulnerable," he said.

"Yes…?"

"There aren't very many of my kind, Tara. We can't afford to be vulnerable to yours."

"But *you* were tonight," she countered with surety.

"Yes." He met her gaze squarely, not trying to hide this truth from her. "You said you didn't understand what was happening between us, Tara. Neither did I."

"And do you now?" she asked.

"No."

She raised a hand to his cheek, touched it lightly, then dropped her hand back down. He didn't know what the gesture meant, but it saddened him immeasurably.

He cut the pain the only way he could think of, by lowering his lips to hers. He tasted her again, reveled in the feel of her wet satin mouth, the slightly salty tang of the tears she'd shed.

She stirred in his arms and enfolded him to her even closer. Her body lifted to meet his, her long silky legs stretched along his own. And when he pulled his lips from hers, trailing them down to the hollow at the base of her throat, she sighed and cradled his head in her hands.

"Gavin…?"

"Mmm?" He flicked his tongue against the points of her collarbone and smiled a little at her sharp intake of air.

"Why…did you marry *me?*" she asked.

He froze, not wanting to tell her, unable to lie. "Because I wanted you," he said. And that was *not* a lie.

"But why marriage?"

He didn't want to tell her that the Council had ordered her death. "Because I wanted you," he repeated. "Not just for a moment or a time, but for as long as possible."

All true but not wholly the truth. Was this how Jonathan had started? Or had it begun earlier for him too, at the first sight of Charlene, as it had with Gavin's first glance at Tara? Had Jonathan also known he was drowning, losing everything even as he gained so much more?

Was he as rogue as Jonathan? Was he falling in love with this mortal? Even as he asked himself the question, he knew the answer. And understood that his heart, which hadn't known the petty emotions of humankind for more years than he cared to count, beat now with mortal feelings inside. But none of the feelings were petty or small. They were huge and rich and lush.

He wanted to curse Tara for this, and at the same time he wanted to fall down on his knees before her and ask for…ask for something, anything that would make it stop. Or grow.

When he'd rashly decided to defy the Council, he hadn't considered that he would *feel* anything for her, aside from simple lust. Now, although he'd made her safe for a brief time, and perhaps himself, too, for as long as the Council would allow it, he'd brought another sort of death upon himself. His dispassion had died; he had lost his precious detachment, the one gift allowed to his society, for without that careful indifference, their existence would truly be living hell.

He shut his eyes with a fierceness that would have startled him earlier and clutched his hands into fists, denying the rage of emotions springing from his heart, which until a few hours ago had been as dead as dried kindling.

"Are you all right?" Tara asked.

No, he wanted to scream. *Can't you see I'm dying?*

But he wasn't dying. He couldn't die. Yet almost anything would be preferable to this unmitigated agony.

"Gavin...?"

The telephone on the bedside table jangled, startling them both.

Tara reached for it. "Hello?" she answered breathlessly.

Gavin watched her as she sat up a bit and turned away from him. She drew a pillow across her glorious body, hiding it from him. Lowering her voice, she cautiously said, "Everything's fine. No. Yes."

Considering his maelstrom of newfound emotions, he should have expected to feel jealousy. But the truth was, it had been so very long since he'd experienced anything remotely like it that he had no name for the anxiety, hurt, and raw fury that coursed through him when she said, "It's okay, Tom."

It wasn't okay. Nothing was okay. She might have changed her mind about wanting to kill him, but she was killing him nonetheless. Killing him with her laughter, her beautiful body, her tenderness, and now her embarrassment as she talked to her conspirator.

She hung up the phone finally and turned to face him, a blush staining her cheeks. Her eyes widened at something she saw on his face and he tried schooling his features, but knew he hadn't succeeded when she drew back from him a little.

"More signals?" he asked. He wanted to rip that ridiculous pillow away from her and press her back against the bed.

"You challenge the Council like a child playing with fire. You taunt me. You drive me insane and you sit there with your innocent face, looking surprised. How do you think I feel listening to you talking with the man you wanted to have kill me?"

She shocked him into absolute stillness by whipping the pillow from in front of her and flinging it at him. She rose from the bed like a goddess from her throne, every inch of her a study in disdain.

In slow, measured steps, she strode to a closed suitcase on the far side of the room. She unzipped it and reached within to secure something. For half a second, unable to analyze the depth of the anger on her face, Gavin expected her to withdraw a wooden stake.

She closed her eyes for a moment then turned to look at him. Her eyes shone bright and luminous, not with anger, but with a sheen of tears. She tossed a slender book to him. The diary.

"Read that and you'll see why I assumed it was you who killed my sister. She spells out every detail of her love for *you*, Gavin Deveroux, not anyone else. You tell me you can't lie. But let me ask this—why would *she*?"

"Tara—"

"You're safe now." She slid his signet ring from her finger—it came off far too easily, he thought—and set it down on the dresser. "And you're free to go."

"But—"

She didn't wait to hear him out. She walked into the

bathroom and softly closed the door behind her. He heard the snap of the lock and then water running in the shower.

Unsure what he was feeling, he slowly turned the diary over in his hands and opened it to the first page.

When he reached the final segment, in which she described the Exchange, a nearly laughable myth in the Society, he closed the diary and held it tightly in his fist.

The Exchange, he thought. Was it really possible? Had Jonathan and Charlene tried it? Was that what killed her and drove Jonathan into madness?

He turned his head toward the closed bathroom door and thought of the woman on the other side, the woman who had loved him so exquisitely, without reservation or fear. He thought of his *wife*.

If only the Exchange were really possible. If only it were not a dream, a tale whispered to the newly crossed, to let them believe a way back existed.

Because if it did exist, if it were real, then…what? They would be together? He less and she more, but together for a day, a night, equals on all levels?

Chapter 8

Tara leaned against the wall in the shower stall letting the hot water wash all illusions away. Pretty dreams and fantasies swirled away into the drain.

When she'd said she would marry Gavin, and did, she hadn't thought beyond trapping him. And when they'd reached the room, she hadn't thought beyond his touch. But his words to her after the phone call from Tom made clear just how wide the gulf was between them.

She'd opened to him as she'd never done with anyone before. She'd trusted him with her body, her life. Her heart. And he'd still believed her capable of conspiring against him. She hadn't had to tell him the truth, but had wanted no secrets between them. Not after the way he made her feel, not knowing the way she felt about him.

She closed her eyes and gave a low sob. She'd told him she was a lot like her sister. Apparently she was far more like her than she'd even guessed, for she too had fallen for someone not even human.

But did she love Gavin? How could it have happened in such a short time?

And if not love, then what could explain the deep pain she felt now, a pain combined with an enervating lethargy. All she wanted to do was turn back the clock and say, "I don't," or turn it ahead and have this all behind her. Because this not knowing the truth was intolerable.

She prayed that when the water ran cold, when she stepped from the bathroom, he would be gone. And she prayed even more fervently that he'd still be there, waiting for her.

Gavin turned the last page of the diary and closed it with a sigh. He heard the water stop running in the shower; he stood and moved away from the bed, uncertain how to proceed with her. The diary had given him both too much and far too little information.

Charlene had never mentioned Jonathan in the pages of her impassioned diary; she'd hidden the truth from any prying eyes. Except that she'd used those pages to pour out her confusion, her astonishment that such a Society existed, that *vampires* walked among the living.

Through her words, Gavin had seen Jonathan's torture, the slow development of his love. And he'd witnessed Charlene's continued desperate involvement with a man/ creature she would never fully understand.

One line she'd written had stricken him to the very quick:

As I lay beside him today, watching him sleep, I longed to slip inside his dreams, to see what he sees when he closes his eyes and looks so young, so care- free.

That Jonathan had trusted her enough to sleep beside her, to stay with her in the daylight hours, shocked and awed Gavin. And filled him with a longing so intense that it nearly drove him to his knees. He had not slept with another being, one of his own kind or mortal, since the Crossing.

He thought back to the moment in Tara's arms when a tremendous languor had sapped him of strength, of anything but the desire to relax into her embrace and close his eyes and sleep. Now he wished he had. For he might never have the opportunity again.

He had to talk to the Council. He didn't know whether or not to show them the damning diary, for though it could no longer harm Jonathan or Charlene, it could further compromise Tara. And himself, since he was named, however erroneously, within its pages.

But if he failed to report to the Council, then they would come looking for him. And the fact that he'd married Tara might save her for a short while because the Council would grant her the same status as any candidate for Crossing. But without being one of them, her knowledge of the Council made her very dangerous to them. But once the Council turned their wrath on him, nothing short of the Exchange would save her. Nothing. And the Exchange was only a myth.

And in the short time he'd known her, he found he couldn't imagine a world without her in it.

He heard her moving around in the bathroom and suddenly couldn't bear to face her. But neither could he consider leaving her. He moved to the curtains leading to the balcony. He heard the door open as he pulled open the drapes.

"No!" Tara cried out from behind him. He whirled, dragging the curtains shut with the force of his move.

"Oh, my God," she called, rushing toward him. "What have you done?"

"What?"

"The curtains. Gavin, they were the signal to Tom. Half open, then closed again. You've got to get out of here!"

In her agitation, her towel slipped and fell to the floor unheeded. She grasped at his arm, trying to drag him toward the door to the room. "Are you listening to me? He'll be here any second. You've got to hurry!"

She scooped his shirt from the far side of the bed and flung it at him and did the same with his trousers.

"And what about you?" he asked, holding the clothes in his hands.

"What about me? He doesn't care about me. Only you."

"Tara."

She fished his socks from the floor and tossed them back at him, bending to her knees to search for his shoes. He couldn't help the reaction he felt upon seeing her fully exposed this way, wholly unaware of the effect she was having upon him.

"Tara," he said again, more firmly.

She found his shoes and turned, her face flushed after her frantic search. "What!"

"If I didn't kill your sister, and Jonathan didn't..."

"But he must have—"

Gavin shook his head. "Why? Why would he do that? You read the diary, Tara. He *loved* her. She knew that, even if she hid his name by using mine."

"How do we know he really loved her? You said yourself that he was insane."

"Not when she wrote the diary. He went insane when he lost her, when he tried Crossing her over after she was already dead, Tara."

"I don't understand. What difference would that make? Why would that make him insane?"

He struggled for an analogy and came up with a weak one. "That would be like diving into a deep swimming pool with no water in it. There's little hope of survival."

She gazed at him for a long moment. "But how do you know he loved her? That she loved you—*him*—we know, but even she was confused about how he felt about her."

"I know, because she said he slept with her."

"What are you saying, that because he made love to her, it was obvious that—?"

"I didn't say 'made love' to her, Tara. I said we know he *loved* her because he 'slept' with her. Closed his eyes and *slept* with her. Nothing but love could make one of my kind do that."

"That's an interesting bit of cultural enrichment, Gavin, but it doesn't solve anything. Tom is on his way here *right this minute* to *kill* you."

"Don't you see, Tara? If I didn't kill your sister, and Jonathan didn't, that only leaves one person."

She stared at him, wondering. "You're saying Tom killed Charlene."

He didn't even bother to nod.

"That can't be right. The DNA proved it wasn't him that…that, well, ripped her throat."

"No, I told you, Jonathan was trying to bring her over. But *after* she was dead, Tara. *After*."

"You're saying Tom is the one who beat her up."

"Not beat her up, Tara. Beat her to death."

She shook her head. "There would have been some evidence."

"Of what? I took care of most of the so-called evidence. I took the club he beat her with, that was covered in blood,

I took—'' He stopped, aware of her shock. She hadn't known about the weapons used on her sister. She had bought Tom's story, wholesale. And now that he had seen the damning statements in Charlene's diary, he could understand why.

She stood before him, paler than pale, trembling, looking at him with great lost eyes. He flung the clothes to the bed and dragged her into his arms.

"You've got to get out of here," she said again.

"Not without you," he murmured into her hair.

"What are you saying, Gavin?"

"I'm saying I'm not leaving here unless you come with me."

"There's no time," she said. "He'll be here any second."

"And what of that, Tara? I'm not asleep. There's nothing he can do to me. We'll lock the door. What's he going to do, use a chain saw to break it down? I would imagine a few guests would complain."

She leaned against him and he held her tighter, loving the feel of her shaking with laughter in his arms. He wished he could do more and just *love* her, the way Jonathan had loved Charlene. It had driven him mad, but this halfway state was an exercise in insanity all in itself.

"I guess you're right," she muttered and tried to pull away.

If he'd let her go right then, if he'd been thinking of anything other than the way her soft skin felt against his, he would have heard the rustle of someone in the hallway, would have heard the stealthy turning of the doorknob.

Chapter 9

One moment Tara felt marginally at peace in Gavin's arms. The next she'd somehow been transported from leaning against his chest to leaning against his naked back.

Gavin had moved her, but so swiftly that all she'd felt was the slightest whisper of shifting air on her bare skin and a dizzying sense of disorientation.

"So, Gavin. Taking a moment's pleasure before business?"

"What in the hell are you doing here?" Gavin snapped.

"Rushing in where angels fear to tread."

"Get out," Gavin said, but Tara would have sworn it was a growl, for she felt it rumble through him.

She'd fully expected Tom to burst into the room, and was utterly confounded at hearing an unfamiliar and very slow Southern drawl.

"I don't think so, Gavin."

One of Gavin's arms was stretched behind him, holding

her tightly against his back, the other he'd placed out to his right side, half bent upward, as if he were holding an invisible sword. Dazed, she stared at that upraised hand, remembering her own earlier vow for the sword of justice.

She'd been so certain then of what she had to do. Now, standing behind Gavin's protective body, she knew nothing except a desire to keep this unusual man safe from harm.

"I won't let you kill her, Gavin."

A trill of shock worked through her, a frisson that must have communicated itself to Gavin, for he strengthened his hold on her.

"And why is that, Jonathan?"

Jonathan? Charlene's Jonathan? Gavin hadn't lied to her, this Jonathan was real? She felt a staggering relief followed by a sharp consternation.

"I'll tell you why. Because she doesn't deserve to die. Her only crime is that she loved her sister."

Tara needed to look at this man, had to *see* him. She felt a moment's embarrassment at her nudity, but she managed to free one of her arms from Gavin's hold to whisk the edge of the bedspread to cover herself and take a look at their guard.

Just inside the door stood a young man with long, wild dark hair, wilder black eyes, and drawn features. His face was all planes and sorrow, hard and angular, a study in despair. This was Jonathan, who had loved her sister.

"Tara," he said. He seemed not to notice her state of undress; his eyes didn't flick over her but held steady with her own.

She squared her shoulders, unwilling to give in to the urge to cover herself more fully. "Jonathan."

"You know who I am?"

"Gavin told me," she said.

He glanced at Gavin in apparent surprise. "You told her about me? Why?"

Tara didn't wait for Gavin to answer. "Because of the diary."

The young man…the young *vampire,* she reminded herself…turned an anguished gaze in her direction. She could all but feel the weight of his longing. His mouth worked, his face tightened into a grimace, but no words came out.

"Gavin told me it was you Charlene wrote about in the diary, not him."

At that, the young man—though he couldn't really be young, could he?—frowned and ran a hand through his hair much as Gavin had done earlier.

"I didn't remember she kept a diary. Not for a long while. And when I did…it was too late."

"Too late?" she asked.

"You had already let the Council know you had it. You and your sister were so close, surely she told you how dangerous that would be."

Tara felt as if someone had poured icy water over her. Close? She and Charlene hadn't been *close* for years. She must have uttered some strangled sound for he stepped forward a pace, which caused Gavin to raise that seemingly invisible sword even higher.

"Y-you're wrong," Tara said. "Charlene and I weren't close at all."

Jonathan stopped where he was but began to speak to her. "She talked about you all the time. She looked up to you. You had the education. The strength. You took care of you when your parents died. You watched out for her, made sure she was okay, made sure she was *loved.* And when she lied to you, which she said she often did, it was only because she didn't want you to think badly of her."

Tara hadn't known. She'd never known. She'd only heard the recriminations, never words of love and gratitude from her sister.

And even when Charlene had died, when she'd learned of her death, her first thought had been of responsibility, that she'd have to take care of this mess, like all the others. Hearing Jonathan's words, hearing the truth in them, she was stricken with a deep sorrow and an almost overwhelming sense of relief. Her sister had *loved* her.

"Why are you here?" Gavin asked, his voice graveled.

"I told you why," Jonathan burst out, venting his emotions at Gavin. "I know the Council sent you to dispose of Tara. When I couldn't find the diary, I started watching her. Waiting. I knew the moment would come. And I knew they'd send someone after her. I just didn't know it would be you until I saw you leaving the memorial tonight."

"What are you saying, Jonathan? That you've come in from exile to protect your lover's sister?"

"Yes, I have. So...*rogue* that I am, I can still battle you any time, Gavin. I don't want to. God knows I don't. But I will. The Council is wrong, don't you see? Can't you feel it? I'll kill you rather than let you take her life."

Gavin slowly lowered his clenched fist. Then he turned to the bed and reached for the silk shirt he'd tossed aside earlier. He yanked it over his head as he sat down heavily.

"I married her, Jonathan."

"Oh, God," Jonathan answered.

Tara looked first from the man who was her husband, then to her would-be defender and saw that some great understanding had passed between the two of them. One immortal to another, however far they were from their sacred Council.

She was keenly aware of her nudity as it seemed to underscore her sensation of being exposed, left in the cold and the dark.

She turned to Gavin, clutching the spread to her breasts. A thousand questions formed in her mind, but her heart asked the only one that mattered, ''Were you sent to kill me?''

He slipped one leg into his pants, then another before answering. ''Yes,'' he said, not looking at her.

''And when you asked me to marry you…?''

He looked up then, linking their gazes, sending that shock wave of recognition through her. ''I was trying to stave off the inevitable.''

Jonathan stepped closer still. ''But you're one of the knights of the Council. You would never betray them.'' He whipped his face toward her. ''Leave now, Tara Michaels. And never look back.''

She dragged her gaze from Jonathan, the man her sister had loved and apparently died loving. Then she stared at the man sitting on the bed, the man she silently entreated to look at her. If Jonathan had loved her sister and was innocent of her murder, then—was it possible? Could Gavin love Tara?

Did she want him to? She thought of the way his face had looked when he said that Jonathan had *slept* with her sister. The longing, the sorrow. The wonder.

But Gavin hadn't slept with her. And now she could see the strong guilt on him. She'd told him of her plans. Revealed all to him. She'd given him every nuance of herself, and he hadn't told her about the Council wanting her dead.

''Gavin…?''

He looked up at her then. ''Jonathan's telling you the truth. The Council sent me to deal with you. To retrieve Charlene's diary and take care of you.''

So he had intended to kill her. The realization was a painful blow. She released a bitter laugh. "You've done both, in a way, haven't you?"

To her great surprise, he smiled in response. She'd meant to be deadly sarcastic, not humorous.

Gavin flicked a glance at Jonathan. "Was her sister this feisty?"

Confounding her still further, Jonathan relaxed another notch and nodded. "She had the same fire."

If she'd had shoes on, she might have stomped her foot, but somehow, nude and barefoot, she thought the gesture would lack impact. She hugged herself tighter.

Gavin sighed and shifted his gold-green gaze back to hers. "I thought that if you paired with me...as in *married* paired...the Council would leave you alone for as long as it might take me to get the diary."

"And then?" Tara asked, suddenly cold.

Gavin's eyes shifted to the floor. He stood up and fastened his trousers, not answering. He reached for her dress and handed it to her.

She took the dress automatically. "And then?" she asked again.

"And then he would kill you," Jonathan answered for him. "Or worse, make you one of us. Cursed for all time."

"No," Gavin said.

"That's not what you intended?" she asked, her eyes on him, not on the dress her hands fumbled with.

"Yes...No! At first, yes. Not later."

Jonathan crossed to the side of the room and flopped into one of the easy chairs flanking the bed. "You've gone rogue. Join a club of one."

"Don't say that," Gavin barked, whirling to face the younger man.

Tara slipped her dress over her head and struggled with the buttons that kept sliding through her fingers. She didn't care if she had anything beneath the dress or not; it felt like armor against her bare skin.

Unnerved as she was, she was still vitally aware that Gavin had inadvertently given Tom the signal, the sign that Gavin was asleep and vulnerable, that he could come and kill him at any moment.

Now, shifting her gaze from one tortured man to the other, she wondered fleetingly why she didn't just slip into the other room and allow it to happen.

Guilt, the like of which she'd never before experienced, darted through her at the thought, making her weak and ready to pitch forward. What kind of creature had *she* become, willing to let a man, two men, be killed?

What were the limits within the soul? What were the limits of the *heart?*

She was unaware she'd spoken aloud until she realized that both men...both *vampires*...were staring at her.

Gavin moved as if to take her into his arms and she stepped back. She knew he could have caught her to him. But he didn't. He dropped his hands and stayed where he was, sadness etching his face.

Jonathan remained in his chair, looking at them with a torment she didn't want to fathom.

"Tara...?" Gavin asked.

She made her decision, sweeping her damp hair from her face and squaring her shoulders as if preparing for battle. She had the odd notion that it was to be a battle not for her life, but for her soul.

Gavin thought no woman in heaven, in hell or on earth could look as magnificent as Tara did at that moment.

"It appears we have to take each other on sheer faith."

She chuckled, though her laugh seemed hollow. "I've already said I don't want you killed. And I'm assuming you feel the same way about me."

Gavin choked on a startled laugh. God, this woman was glorious. "Yes," he said, forcing the smile from his lips.

"So. It looks like a case of the lady and the vampires versus the vampire slayer and your Council."

Jonathan let loose a burst of genuine laughter at this and Gavin turned an amazed stare in his old friend's direction. This immortal man's laughter had the same quality that he'd detected in Tara's earlier that night, a single melody, pure and unsullied. There were differences, of course, but the similarities were too close to ignore.

His longtime friend cut the laughter short when Tara leveled her cool stare on him. "The next person that walks in that door," she said, pointing in that direction, "will not stop to ask questions."

Gavin wanted to tell her that she needn't fear the mortal, Tom. That man was less than nothing. He wanted to tell her that he felt as if he had all the magic in the universe at his fingertips. Because of her.

Gazing at her standing there, barefoot, wet-haired, and wearing nothing but a bit of silk material that clung to the damp spots of her body, Tara personified Athena. The goddess. His goddess.

And she was so incredibly vulnerable. She had no concept of the forces at work against her. But her sheer naiveté augmented his own strength. Because damned though he already was, he knew to the very depths of his doomed soul that he wouldn't allow anything to harm her now. Or ever.

He turned to Jonathan, a friend he'd helped to cast out, a person he'd abandoned in the midst of the kind of pain he hoped he would never know, and sought help from him. "Can you stay with her? I'm going to the Council."

"It'll do no good," Jonathan said, shaking his head. "Better to run with her and hide."

Gavin scowled at him. "I'll make them see the truth."

Jonathan issued a bitter snort. "I was one of the Council, remember?"

"I'll explain."

"What? What will you explain? That you didn't follow their edict? That you slept with a mortal?"

"I didn't sleep with her," Gavin said.

"No? But you want to, don't you? And once you cross that barrier there is no going back to the way we were. And the Council will know that the minute they see you. It's in your voice, in the way your eyes soften when you look at her."

"Tara won't be there."

"It won't matter," Jonathan said. "You'll still be exiled and they will just send someone else to kill her."

"I'll take the diary with me."

"And do what, burn it, tear it into shreds before their eyes? Do you honestly think that will impress any of them? You were like them just a short time ago. Would such a spectacle have impressed you?"

"I would have wanted to know the truth," Gavin said, but he knew his voice sounded uncertain. The look of scorn on Jonathan's face told him just how uncertain.

"I was in love with Charlene. I didn't know what I was feeling, what I was experiencing in the release of those emotions. But when I lost her…you didn't exactly search for any truth, did you, Gavin?"

"I didn't know," Gavin said, starkly honestly. Guilt smote him. He'd dragged Jonathan from his lover's battered body and whisked him from the house, then had cast him from the Society. Left him alone and insane.

"No, you didn't. It's funny, I should hate you for that, but I don't," Jonathan said. "I just feel sorry for you now, because you're trying to be in both worlds. They won't allow that, Gavin. And you want to know the worst part? You won't be able to allow it either. You're a man caught between now. Forsaken in both."

"I've got to try," he said. But was he trying for Tara's sake or out of some desire to travel between both worlds as Jonathan had implied?

"While you two are arguing, Tom is on his way up here," Tara said urgently, touching his arm only to pull her hand away as if his skin burned her. Certainly hers had branded him.

"He must have missed the signal, Tara. He'd have been here some time ago. And you forget, I'm not asleep. I'm not vulnerable to him. Nor is Jonathan."

He turned back to the one being who understood him probably more than any other now. "Jonathan, will you stay with her?" he asked again, hating himself because of his own guilt, because he feared his former friend was right about the Council, right about himself. Nonetheless, he had to try. No matter what happened to him, Tara would never be safe unless he tried. "Please."

Jonathan studied him for what seemed an eternity, then finally nodded and stood from his chair. "Not for you, Gavin. Your notion of loyalty goes against the grain. But for Charlene." He turned his gaze to Tara. "Because she loved you."

When Gavin saw the film of tears blur Tara's eyes, he wanted to go to her, to draw her into his arms and comfort her. But he couldn't, because everything Jonathan had said about him was true. And nothing he could say or explain about the past would make it less so. But he did pick up his ring she'd left on the dresser.

"What time is it?" he asked.

"Just three hours before dawn," Jonathan answered in the way of their kind, no hour or tracking of the clock, only the sun.

"I'll persuade them," he said.

He was aware of Tara's understanding. She didn't ask what they meant, not because she knew for certain, but she suspected. She met his gaze and he knew she understood that he was leaving Jonathan with her to protect her from Tom. He took her limp hand and pushed his ring back onto her finger.

"I can feel you as long as you wear this," he said. He felt as if something were obstructing his throat. "Please keep it on."

"Gavin—"

"Please, Tara."

She looked at him, her eyes still bright with unshed tears, however much her gaze was steady and true. "On one condition," she said, her voice graveled and rough.

And he thought how like her it was to issue a challenge in response. A would-be chuckle worked through him. "And what is that?" he asked.

"That you come back to me."

At her words, he felt as if all the swords in heaven and hell stabbed through his heart.

"Go," Tara said, curling her hand around his ring. "Jonathan and I...we'll talk about Charlene."

He nodded and turned toward the balcony exit, not taking his eyes from hers. She blinked at the direction he was taking and he half smiled. "Three hours is a long time for our kind, Tara."

"Be careful," she said.

"Take care of her," he said to Jonathan gruffly.

"I will," Jonathan said.

"And if I don't come back...?"

Jonathan nodded.

"What does that mean?" Tara asked. "What are you saying? They wouldn't do anything to you, would they? Aside from this exile thing?"

He couldn't bear to look at her with a lie in his eyes. He swiftly stepped out onto the balcony and took a deep breath of the chilled October air. Drinking in the semidarkness of the city, he thought about Tara as he stepped into the night.

And he wondered if he would ever see her again, know her touch, taste her honeyed warmth.

Far away he seemed to hear her calling to him, if only in his own wish-filled thoughts, "Come back to me."

For the first time in centuries, Gavin wished he knew how to pray.

Chapter 10

"What did he mean when he said that about not coming back?" Tara asked Jonathan.

He looked at her steadily for a long moment. "It's close to dawn."

She knew the color had already drained from her face, but felt it drop yet another notch lower. All the myths she'd ever heard about vampires bursting into flame, screaming at the sight of the dawn's light, streaked through mind. But she managed to ask steadily enough, "And that's dangerous?"

He gave her a wry look and smiled a little. "Dangerous. Yes, you could safely say that."

"But this Council of yours, they wouldn't kill him, would they?"

Jonathan shrugged. "Exile has always been the threat of the Council."

"Gavin said it had happened twice."

Jonathan frowned and shifted his eyes from hers. "The other was a long time ago. Before I crossed. Long before Gavin did."

"You're older?"

He chuckled. "Strange for you to imagine? Yes. I'm much 'older' than Gavin, if you consider the dates of our birth. But you have to understand we don't exactly consider age after the Crossing."

"You and Gavin were friends," Tara stated, but it was really a question. She wanted to understand what had happened between the men that would allow Gavin to reject a friend of long standing merely because he'd fallen in love with a mortal woman.

Jonathan took some time to answer. "Yes. Friends. As much as any of us can be. You could say that we took to one another right away. He was like I was with the Crossing. Needing it somehow. Some are taken unaware and fight it. Not us. We'd both been unhappy as mortals and I think it was a relief to shut out those emotions that created the unhappiness."

Tara settled on the bed, her heart pounding fearfully. Jonathan was telling her about the eradication of all human emotion. Something many people in pain had prayed for at times, but, more thankfully, could never accomplish. Except Jonathan and Gavin and their strange Society had done such a thing.

She didn't know how to prompt Jonathan to continue, didn't want to seem too curious or too horrified at the concept of what he termed "the Crossing."

He drew a deep breath and let it out in a shuddering sigh. "We seemed alike in so many ways, Gavin and I, in those early days. And yet we were fundamentally different. I have always despised the Society, even though I became a member of the High Council. Gavin embraced it. It became his reason for living, if anyone could ever call this hell a life.''

"Is it such a hell?" Tara asked softly, thinking of Gavin's desire that she never know, and wishing she'd been brave enough to ask Gavin himself. Somehow it was far easier and less painful to ask the questions of the man who had loved her sister, had gone into exile for her.

"A hell? It is *the* hell. Never to know a gentle touch, or see love in a woman's eyes. Never to hold a child and feel awe or joy. To walk through a beautiful garden and not be stirred by its wildness or its serenity. To eat but never savor, to sleep but never dream. To ache only from mindless hunger, not from poetry or art or a summer morning.''

"But he does feel…" Tara began, only to trail away. Gavin's touch had been as gentling as a healer's or as rousing as all the forces of nature combined.

"Does he? Are you so certain?" Jonathan asked.

She answered from the deepest depths of her heart. "Yes, I'm certain," she said finally. And she was sure she was right. She had to be right.

Jonathan shrugged. "Perhaps. I can't imagine it, not from Gavin, the perfect example of the High Council. But maybe you have touched something in him."

"Why were you surprised that he'd married me?" she asked.

"Because it's forbidden. Because it links you to him for all time. Brands you."

"So why is he worried about the Council? If he's branded me, as you call it."

"Because by marrying you, he risks everything. Exile. Even what life he has."

"But how am I a threat to the Council?"

Jonathan met her eyes squarely. "You, every woman like you...like Charlene...you are all threats to the Society."

"Why? I don't understand."

"Because you're strong. You're vibrant. You are everything we are not. All our immortality, all our powers pale by comparison."

"Gavin made me feel like that somehow," she mused.

"Ahh. Then you may be right. Maybe he has forsaken the Council."

"Which will put him in even greater jeopardy," she said, knowing it would be true.

He neither nodded nor acknowledged her words and this frightened her worse than a simple "yes" might have done.

"Has he talked to you of the Exchange?" he asked, not looking at her now.

"No," she said, but she remembered the final passage in Charlene's diary had referred to it. "What is the Exchange?"

"A myth. Just a myth."

"Charlene mentioned it in her diary."

He shot her a swift and agonized glance, then dropped his eyes. "It was too late," he said. "Too late for anything. I even tried bringing her over to save her, but I was too late."

"Did Tom...beat her to death?"

"I don't know. She was alone when I found her. Her beautiful body...her life... I was too late," he said.

His inability to describe more told Tara all too clearly what he'd found when he'd entered her sister's house. She'd seen the harrowing police photos, which had allowed her to identify her sister without having to face the horror in the flesh. She'd heard Tom's tearful description of finding Tara with Gavin...or Jonathan.

"This Exchange thing would have changed her?" she asked.

"And me."

Tara felt a chill run down her back. "How?"

He waved a hand, as if in anger. "It's a myth, Tara. Just a myth. Gavin knows that."

"But you were willing to try it."

"I was in love with your sister."

He didn't have to say anything more, the implication was obvious. He'd been in love and willing to try anything. Gavin, by implication, wasn't in love with his wife.

"What does the Exchange involve?"

"Tara, it doesn't matter. It's only a myth! Don't you see, we were grasping at straws—"

"Tell me, Jonathan. Please."

"Why? What difference will it make?"

"Because I love Gavin."

He drew his breath in on a hiss and raked her face with fevered eyes. "How can you love him?"

She smiled a bit sadly, and with a small measure of humor. "The heart knows in seconds."

"You don't know what you're doing. You're dazzled—confused."

"Did my sister love you, Jonathan?"

"How I wanted to believe she did."

"Did you love her?"

"Oh, yes. I loved her more dearly than life itself."

"Then tell me. Please. If only because it will give me something to hope for."

One second Jonathan was leaning against the dresser, then suddenly, abruptly he was sitting beside her on the bed and taking her balled fist into his palm. She uttered a startled cry and jerked back from him.

And he was just as suddenly and frighteningly back at the dresser, his arms crossed and looking perfectly relaxed. "You don't understand what we are. What you will become a part of. If the myth about the Exchange is true, you would be as we are. The laws of physics will no longer apply."

"And he would be able to what…to die?"

"To age. To have mortality like any one of you," he said, then added reflectively, "Gavin obviously didn't reveal any of his powers to you. Which, in its way, is probably the greatest compliment he could have paid you."

"He moved me behind him when you came in the room. And he what…flew from the balcony?"

"When I was beside you a moment ago, it startled you, made you jump. Why? Not because you are frightened of me, I think, but because you knew it was a movement not quite right. Something inhuman in it. We can move more quickly than the human eye can register. And we can do more than this. Much more. But all of this power is predicated on the taking of mortal life. And in order to do that, we are shut off from feeling."

"But you fell in love with my sister," she said, trying to understand him so that she could understand Gavin.

"Yes."

"How?"

He smiled sadly. "How does anyone fall in love? I saw her in the elevator. And she smiled at me."

Tara shivered a little at that. She'd often told Charlene her trusting smile would get her in trouble one day. The smile slipped from her face. She'd had no idea how prophetic that admonition would prove to be.

"If you don't have the emotions…"

"Don't you understand, Tara? We have them. We have every one, but they are so hidden behind the mask of these powers that we are safe from them. The whole Society believes themselves immune to any but the primal urges of thirst and hunger. And lust.''

She found herself shaking her head, everything in her knowing that Gavin had not come to her in mere primal need. He'd made love to her. Exquisitely, passionately. With true emotion.

''And you found out that you had more? That you could love?''

''Yes.''

''I still don't understand why this would be a crime.''

''If more of us gave in to those emotions, there would be no control in the Society. All the members would be vulnerable to you mortals. It would be like an addiction, an obsession spreading throughout our kind. Like children, they would try outdoing themselves in experiencing new and different emotions. Some would likely kill out of rage or hatred. Others would find a way to suicide, because they wouldn't be able to tolerate their hideous existence any longer. And those like me would fall in love with a fiery little artist who created magic with a simple charcoal pencil.''

''And like me with Gavin,'' she said, wondering why she could so easily admit it to Jonathan when she'd been wholly unable to say anything remotely like the words to Gavin himself. ''Tell me about the Exchange.''

Jonathan studied her for a long moment, then sighed heavily. ''You'll remember that there are no guarantees?''

''There's no guarantee that Gavin will even come back before dawn,'' she said quietly.

Jonathan sighed again and this time slowly moved to sit beside her on the broad bed. ''According to lore, it's very dangerous, because it requires a total baring of the soul.

Not many humans can endure this, and not many of the Society would ever willingly attempt such a thing.''

"Tell me," she urged, remembering that time was running out.

"The first real step involves your willingness to die for him. Are you willing, Tara? Are you really willing, on the basis of knowing him one night and knowing what he really is. Are you willing to *die* for Gavin?"

Chapter 11

"Oh, hell, Gavin, if she's all that special, just give her the Crossing and bring her over. Have done with it. She's only a mortal, after all."

Gavin curled his hand into a fist, then forced himself to relax. His only hope to persuade the members of the Council to leave Tara alone was to remain calm and seemingly indifferent.

He tossed Charlene's diary onto the long table surrounded by the twelve members of the governing body of the Society.

One of them picked up the slender book, flipped through it in a flash and handed it to another. As the diary passed around the table, faster than the single ticking of a clock, Gavin was struck by the difference of time between his world and Tara's. In hers everything seemed to move slowly, each movement of the second hand on a clock having significance, each touch all the more weighty because of it. In his, centuries meant nothing.

The candles in the wall sconces along the cavern walls cast eerie shadows on the faces of the members, making people Gavin had known for years seem strangers. Or perhaps it had nothing to do with the shadows, but rather some indefinable difference within himself?

The Council's table, so familiar to him, should have looked out of place in the bowels of such caverns well beneath the ground. But somehow the grandeur of the caverns served to make the High Council's meeting seem even more important. And with his new vision, he saw it as mere trappings, pomp for the sake of pomp, not because anything in the Council warranted such decorum.

He'd not had to arrive at a specific time, an appointed date. He'd called the meeting of the Council as he hurled himself from the balcony of Tara's room. Now that he was here, in this somber, cold place, the sound of Tara's laughter lingered in his mind, and he remembered the way she'd sighed at his kiss, had moved beneath his hand.

Now, because of Tara, he *lived* as he never dreamed of living before the Crossing.

"You're telling us that this Tara Michaels just handed this diary over, that her challenge was more in the nature of a gift than a threat?" one of them asked.

"Exactly," Gavin said, feeling a staggering relief that he'd managed to convey that much to this emotionless group, considering the extent of his own fears and worry.

One of the women, Alana, one who had made the Crossing only a few years after he had, leaned back in her chair. "And what magic did this woman, this *mortal*, use to persuade our Gavin to believe her pathetic little story?"

It was a question whose answer was fraught with danger. If he spoke truthfully, they could swoop down upon Tara as swiftly as vultures. Unless he told them he'd married her, which would damn him in their eyes; he would be exiled, not maddened like Jonathan, but outside the security of the Society, and therefore fighting them at every turn.

And wouldn't that stance damn him in his own eyes? In his own heart? Was Jonathan right about him? Did he need them so, did he need to cling to the Society so as not to *feel?*

"Gavin," Alana said. "Tell us the truth. Was she as delectable as her kind always are? Did she dance to your piping willingly?"

A surge of raw hatred rose in him. He thought of Tara, of her indescribable sweetness, of her open, honest avowal of her feelings.

He said coldly, "You want the truth, Alana? I'll tell you. I knew you—*we*—had made a mistake the moment I saw Tara. Everything about her screams truth. She only wanted to give the diary over to us. You have it now. So, *leave her be.*"

Alana laughed, a discordant, harsh laughter that fell on Gavin's ear like the grating of a saw against metal.

"You fool, Gavin. Did you think you could lie to us and get away with it?"

"No," he said simply. He'd only tried staving off the inevitable.

He thought of all the years he'd faithfully served the Council and all the times he'd enjoyed Alana's sneering at mortals. They had laughed together at the fallibility of humankind. They had played a game for fifty years or more, of finding the most damning quotes about their frailer cousins.

Now he could only think of one frail woman who held all the power of love in her slender hands. Every second he was away from her left her vulnerable. He *had* to make the Council understand. And, at that precise moment, Gavin knew where his allegiance rested—in Tara's soft hands.

Alana's eyes narrowed and she moved forward in her chair. "Let us understand. You went to dispatch her and get her sister's diary. We've got the diary now, yes. But the mortal lives. We'll have to send someone else. Someone who can do the job."

"No!" Gavin's hand hit the Council table, making all the members start.

In his anger and fear for Tara, Gavin forgot he'd ever worried about his own exile from this vile Council, from the Society they governed. Only Tara held any importance for him now. Now and forever.

"What's to stop us, Gavin?" Alana sneered.

"She is my *wife*," he said coldly, slowly, allowing his words and their impact to sink in.

Alana half rose from her chair and Gavin swore he saw more than mere righteousness in her action. It wasn't hunger, need, or even anger that fueled her ire. It was something else.

She rested her hands on the table and leaned forward, her face a study in fury. But her voice was ice-cold as she asked, "Did you forget, in the heat of her arms, the touch of her lips upon you…in that glory, did you forget that she was a toy, a morsel to be consumed, nothing more?"

He'd had enough. "You're the toy, Alana. A plastic

nothing, without heart, without joy. Without compassion. You've forgotten what it feels like."

"*Feels* like, Gavin?"

Gavin raked his eyes across every member at the table. "*Feels* like. Yes…*feels*. You've all forgotten. Or are trying to forget still. And yet, you all know what I mean when I say the word. Somewhere deep inside you. You may not admit it. You may not like it. I didn't at first. And maybe I still don't. But I'm not crazed, as Jonathan was when Tara's sister was murdered and I exiled him for you. I'm wholly aware and alert. I married Tara Michaels to keep her from your filthy hands."

Even Alana looked shocked at his outburst. The other members shifted uncomfortably. One of them even looked at the watch on his wrist, as if seeking a way out by calling a halt to the proceedings due to the nearness of dawn. Except it wasn't anywhere near dawn where they were. In the cavern there was no day or night.

It was the safest of all safe places for his kind. And he was rejecting it. He felt the stunning weight of such an action course through him, but it meant nothing in comparison with the lure of Tara's laughter.

"And as long as she wears my ring, she is protected," he said, staking a claim he thought never to do.

"Only as long as your heart still beats," Alana purred, looking at his chest with obvious menace in her cold glare.

Amazingly, he chuckled at the cheap threat. She had no idea what danger really was. Danger was laying his heart bare. Alana's threat seemed comical in the wake of the metamorphosis he'd experienced in Tara's arms.

By the startled expressions on the Council members'

faces, he suspected his laugh had carried a note or two that struck them differently than it once had.

He'd wondered, before he came to them, if he could possibly fully accept an exiled status. Now, contrasting them with Tara, with the effortless magic she wove and the feelings he had for her, he knew that to be an exile with her for eternity was infinitely preferable to spending another ten minutes with his kind. But he still had to ensure her safety from them.

"John," he said, turning his gaze to a man he'd deemed a friend for some two hundred years. "You crossed when your wife died at childbirth, taking the child with her. Some part of you still longs for her. If you take that pain and embrace it, she'll live for you again. Not in the flesh, but in your heart."

John looked away, not thoughtfully as Gavin would have wished, but as if in embarrassment that one of their own was making such a spectacle of himself.

"And Jason, your sons were killed in a hunting accident and you blamed yourself. You ran blindly into the night, seeking anything that would spare you that kind of grief. And what did you find? Alana. She gave you the Crossing. And you didn't scream inside anymore. You were at peace. Or are you? Did your sons mean so little to you that you can consign them to being mere *toys* for such as we have become?"

And without pause he turned to the only member of the Council standing. "And you, Alana, rejected by your lover on your wedding night. Oh yes, you're the quintessential seductress. No one can resist you now, can they? Even if it is only dark magic and, like the black widow, you kill those you take. But what of the warmth, the love? Isn't that what you really crave? Not to seduce but to be seduced? Not to take, but to be loved. And—''

A sudden, agonizing fiery ball of pain shot through him, choking his words, making him stagger slightly.

Tara!

Tara was in dire trouble. Every fiber of his being screamed with the need to go to her.

Chapter 12

Gavin, Tara called inwardly, knowing even as she sent the cry that it was no use.

Time seemed to have taken on a different shape and form in the last hours before dawn. It wasn't just that her entire world had turned upside down, it seemed the whole universe had dramatically altered all its known laws. What was wrong had shifted to right, what had been true was now a shattered lie.

One moment Jonathan had been telling her about the Exchange, asking her if she was willing to die for Gavin. And as if her hesitant answer had sparked a tempest in the room, the door to the hotel room burst from its hinges.

Faster even than the door bursting in, Jonathan had whipped her behind him, sending her sprawling from the bed. But not before she'd seen who entered.

If she'd had time to think about it, she would have

assumed the forceful latecomer to be Gavin; he'd left that way and it made a macabre sense that he would come back via the same unusual route.

But it wasn't Gavin, it was Tom.

"Tom!" she called out. "Stop. Wait."

But all her fear turned to cold, dark despair as he looked at her and sneered, "She was mine and they took her."

She stared at the man who at one time had been her sister's fiancé, a man she'd believed wronged. Now she saw him for what he was, a man capable of murder, a man who had talked her into plotting murder herself.

"Tom," she said urgently, trying to force him to listen to her, to understand the humanity that was their birthright, the birthright of all them, vampire and mortal. "You don't have to do this."

But his eyes were overbright, filled with anger and a wildness she thought never to see in a human's eyes. He turned that gaze from her to Jonathan, who stood between them, arms outstretched slightly, as if ready for battle.

"I suppose he told you he didn't rip Charlene's throat out."

Tom was standing just inside the room. He held something in his hands, something hidden in one fist and a strange-looking mallet in the other. Tara caught only a brief glimpse of the weapon, seeing odd carvings on it.

Tom stared at Jonathan. "You!" he cried out in a voice that all but deafened Tara. Even Jonathan flinched.

But Jonathan straightened immediately, a look of all too human rage on his features. "You claimed to love her but you killed her!"

"She was mine," Tom yelled.

And in his eyes Tara saw what she should have known

all along, what her sister had probably known all along. Tom was mad.

Gavin, she implored silently, *where are you?*

She felt the slightest movement from Jonathan, but the mirror four feet away from her suddenly shattered, sending silvery shards raining out into the room.

Tara screamed and covered her head instinctively as glass flew.

Tom gave a howl of pure rage. Some of the ire drained from his face, though the madness remained. He said to her, almost conversationally, "I'd have spared you, you know. If you hadn't lied to me."

Tara couldn't have spoken, she was too frightened. Now as much of what Jonathan might do as of Tom. *Gavin,* she called silently.

Jonathan took another step between them. "You are a dead man. If you have any last prayers, say them now."

Tom laughed derisively. "You think I didn't come protected? I came to kill you. And Deveroux. You should all be dead, every one of you. You're all evil."

"Yet you're the one who killed Charlene."

"I only saved her from a worse fate!" Tom yelled. "You're demon spawn."

"And you're not?" Jonathan growled.

Unseen by both mortal and vampire, Tara slipped Gavin's ring from her finger and with more than a pang of regret, let it slip silently to the floor.

"She was *mine,*" Tom yelled at Jonathan. "You used your powers to steal her from me."

"Charlene…" Tara murmured, dragging herself to her knees.

Tom whirled on her. "And *you,* you defend this monster. You *marry* one of them. And *bed* him."

Tara didn't bother to point out that Tom had urged her to do whatever it took to entrap Gavin. Reasoning with madness was a fool's errand.

"Did you love her?" Jonathan asked Tom softly.

Tom gave a half shriek. "You dare to ask me about love? *You?*"

"I loved her," Jonathan said, but his words were drowned in Tom's scream of rage.

Gavin dragged at the air, scarcely having breathed during his ultra-rapid flight to reach Tara's side. With his acute powers of hearing, he caught everything uttered within the hotel room...including Tara's uneven breathing.

Relief flooded through him, even as everything in him cried out that she was not yet safe.

He was aware that Jonathan thought himself invincible against this mortal, and under most circumstances, he would have been. But Tom was insane and therefore not to be underestimated. And the man had read Charlene's diary and therefore knew many of their kind's vulnerabilities.

With use of his own stealthy powers, he turned the knob of the door so swiftly its movement wouldn't be detected, and rapidly took assessment of the room.

Tara knelt on the floor, amidst shards of the broken mirror. Her wide, frightened eyes were on Tom. Jonathan stood only inches away from her, and all his concentration was on the mortal also, so much so that even his augmented senses didn't perceive Gavin behind him.

Tom screamed out in rage and tensed for a lunge at Jonathan. Before he could so much as begin to execute

the leap, Gavin whipped into the room and scooped Tara
up into his arms and out of the madman's way.

Tara released a short shriek as Gavin swung her up
and onto the bed and whirled toward the leaping man. A
shot of what felt like lightning jolted through him, throwing him back against the wall.

Tom hadn't been lunging, he'd been tensed to raise the
object in his hands. It was no simple, hand-pounded silver cross, nor any ornate blessed object from a church,
though it certainly resembled both of those things. It was
an antique *crosier,* a headpiece from a bishop's staff, the
only icon truly able to harm one of the Society. It harmed
them not because it had belonged to any bishop, but because its unique shape and many layers of silver literally
robbed one of the Society of their manifold powers. It
had been designed by their enemies long before Chris-
tianity. Its magical shape represented the essence of life
itself, the elements. The sharp point at its base could be
used as a dagger if need be. As a collective, they had
long ago rid the world of them, safely ensconcing them
in church museums and the like. And yet, this Tom, this
killer of their kind incredibly had one in his possession.

He wielded it triumphantly, capturing the light from
the overhead lamp and driving pure agony into the hearts
of the two vampires.

"Tom!" Gavin dimly heard Tara cry out. "Stop it,
Tom! Oh, God, what are you doing?"

But Tom ignored her pleas and this time, did lunge,
the object in his other hand rising only to come down
directly into Jonathan's helpless chest.

A look of supreme surprise crossed Jonathan's face.
He raised his eyes beyond Tom's shoulder and seemed
to smile even as he slumped against the killer.

Almost as swiftly as one of the Society might have moved, Tara leapt from the bed. She threw her full weight against Tom, unbalancing him, dragging him back against the shard-covered dresser.

Terror for her safety infused a modicum of life back into Gavin's veins, yet still he couldn't move. He could only watch helplessly as Tara's momentum propelled the two mortals to the floor in a crash. Tara's leap on the madman had an unexpected side effect beyond stopping the *crosier's* deadly control. When she pushed Tom off balance, his hand had still been gripped around the odd wooden spike he'd plunged into Jonathan's chest and at his slip backward he'd brought the symbol-laden spindle with him, only now its shaft was covered with Jonathan's blood.

In terror and shock, Gavin watched Tom wrestle with Tara and then raise the spike, fighting with her to aim its deadly tip in her direction. Released from the incredible agony and lethargy that the *crosier* had placed on him, Gavin staggered across the room to save the only thing that meant anything on earth to him. *Tara.*

He cried out her name in desperation, stumbling over a moaning Jonathan, summoning every bit of his latent strength to reach her side before that deadly spindle could enter her body.

Even as he exerted his inhuman speed, he knew he was too late. In midair, he saw Tara's head jerk back and felt more than heard the cry of pain escape her lips. His own heart torn asunder, he plucked her from Tom's grasp and with a sweep of his hand flung the madman across the room to crash into the wall, not caring whether the man lived or not.

"Tara," Gavin said imploringly.

She moaned and her eyes fluttered open to meet his. Cradling her in his arms, he held her close to his chest, trying desperately to staunch the flow of her life force with only his hand. He was a creature of such power, but all the power in his touch couldn't heal the one human he loved, the one human with the power to mend his shattered heart.

"No," he murmured, "You can't die. Listen to me, Tara."

Dimly he heard Tom moan and raised his head for a renewed conflict. But Jonathan reached the man first, his wounds mortal but his need for revenge stronger.

There was no battle, no struggle. One moment the madman Tom was alive, and the next he was gone. There would be no Crossing for him. And by the looks of Jonathan, his time had also come. Gavin could only stare at his onetime friend with bleak supplication.

"Bring her over," Jonathan said.

"I can't," Gavin said and his voice caught on a sob.

"You must," Jonathan gasped, slumping to the floor. "She'll die."

"No," Gavin said. "I'd never condemn her to the dark world we live in. We were wrong. The Crossing doesn't dull pain, it dulls life. To live without love is to be truly dead."

"But you have love now. She will still be alive."

"Will she? Or will she be as Alana is?"

"You have to try."

"No!" Gavin growled. "Never!"

Jonathan coughed and slumped still lower. "The Exchange. While she lives…she's already proven…she's willing to die for you. The Exchange, Gavin. It's your only…hope."

Gavin felt a great stillness work through him. He felt as if every pore in his body quieted, questing for the truth. Would it work? Was it more than a myth? Did Tara's salvation lie in the Exchange, the ultimate mating of mortal and vampire?

"It could kill you, too," Jonathan gasped out. "A church..."

If he was killed in the Exchange, and yet still brought Tara back from the brink of death, he would die happily. Oh, he would die willingly for her. He rose to his feet in the fluid motion peculiar to his kind and held her tightly clasped against him, silently urging her to keep breathing, to stay with him just a while longer.

He glanced down at Jonathan. As if his old friend could read his thoughts, he merely lifted a pale, pale hand and whispered, "Go...now!"

Gavin strode from the room in that swift movement that had caused so many people over the centuries to tell tales of the Society's ability to shape-shift or to fly. He ran through the corridor, into the stairwell and down the flights of stairs.

He didn't know where a church might be in this vast and busy city. But most of the major hotels had a chapel. It would have to do. He had no time. Tara had no time.

He plunged into a smallish chamber off one side of the many ballrooms on the main floor, trusting his instincts for danger to lead him to a place of human worship. Suddenly he was inside, in a church-like room, a place forbidden to him since the day of the Crossing.

Where Gavin expected a tasteless display so common in a city that made quick ceremonies of marriage the standard, the hotel's chapel was calm and quiet in its decor. But he felt no sense of peace in the surroundings of oak paneling and neutral carpet.

Every icon in the non-denominational chapel lashed at him, making him struggle to maintain his hold on Tara's fragile body.

If he'd prayed on the way to what he now believed his fool's errand to the Council, he pleaded with all the gods possible now. And to one in particular that he'd forsaken centuries before when he'd willingly embraced the Society.

He staggered up the aisle between some six wood pews strung with white ribbon, clutching a too-still Tara in his arms. The altar at the front of the chapel was raised slightly on a rounded dais and had been draped with white frothy material that seemed to waft to the floor like cascading clouds.

He stumbled over the dais, the pain in his body crippling him, and he rolled, but never once let loose of his precious burden. "No," he called out, coming to rest in the soft silk of the altar cloth. Horrifying him, he saw a streak of red stain the purity of the white curtain.

"No," he said again, but this time an entreaty against the worst that could happen. "Let her live. Please, God. Let her live. Take me. Please."

And incredibly, he felt tears upon his cheeks, scalding him, choking him, blinding him.

"The Exchange," he heard someone say behind him, and for a moment, thought it was God answering his prayer. He looked up, blinking away the hot tears and took in the sight of the Council standing in a semi-circle behind him.

He couldn't understand why they were there, couldn't understand anything beyond the pain of losing Tara.

Alana held something out to him, and almost automatically, he reached up a hand to take it. His palm was smeared with Tara's life force. Alana gently placed his own signet ring into his hand and folded it shut.

"Put it on her finger," she said.

Gavin stared at her for a moment before complying, trying to make her remarkable presence in the chapel make some semblance of sense. But it didn't.

The rest of the council was silent, solemn. The collection of starkly beautiful people were obviously fighting against tremendous pain and masking it with pure concentration on the woman in Gavin's arms. They had come to help him as he'd requested. They'd come to help with the Exchange. He didn't know why they had chosen this course, and didn't care. He only felt a surge of hope sweep through him, strengthening him.

With shaking fingers, he slid the heavy ring on Tara's finger, kissing it into place.

Chapter 13

Gavin felt a fever of desperation flaming him. Each second seemed an eternity.

In the heart that only a day before he'd have sworn he didn't have, couldn't have, Gavin screamed out against the injustice, agonized over the part he had played in Tara's torment. He wanted to die from the pain, yet perversely clung to the hope inherent in the Exchange.

And then, as if she were awake, Gavin felt Tara's presence, a soft warm touch, as if she stroked his face. The agonizing relief made him dizzy.

"She's alive," he gasped out.

"How do you know?" one of them asked.

"I don't know. I feel it. She has my ring again."

Several of the council members nodded.

"It is true," Gavin heard Alana say wonderingly. "Our kind can have emotions."

John nodded.

* * *

Tara felt a burning in her hand and a steady, gnawing pain in her heart. The sensations were made all the stranger and more perplexing because she couldn't seem to open her eyes to discover the cause. She felt oddly warm and cold at the same time, as if enveloped by strong arms in a freezing wind.

She could hear voices as if from far away, frightening voices, intoning words she didn't understand, words that led her away from the pain eating at her, but somehow not comforting her. Only the arms around her had that ability.

She wished they were Gavin's arms, holding her as he'd held her when they married. But she'd last seen Gavin driven to his knees by a strange object in Tom's hand, had seen Jonathan slain by the wooden spike Tom had wielded with such ferocity and madness.

Gavin. Despair swept through her, seeming to crush what little spirit she felt she still possessed. *Gavin.* A monster in the world's eyes yet the most tender of husbands. A creature of night, but one who had shown her the sweetest of light.

She wanted to quell the voices murmuring their mysterious words, to tell them to go away and let her drift, remembering Gavin. But she couldn't summon any words to shut them out. She wanted to look at whatever was burning her hand so, but couldn't drag her eyes open. Was she dead?

If Gavin was gone, as she was sure he must be, then she didn't want to be alive. What a string of terrible losses, Charlene, Jonathan, Gavin…and now herself. What a waste of lives, human or otherwise. The biggest weight being the loss of Gavin. He saw himself as unfeeling, monstrous, as an evil force. He was the exact opposite.

She wished she'd told him, ached to turn back the hands of time and let him know how much she'd learned about him, about herself, in their short time together. A time that had reshaped her entire existence into one of emotion, meaning…life.

"Be as one. With the mingling of the blood, be as one."

She struggled against lethargy that held her fast, hearing a choir of voices that seemed to compel her to do something, demanded she listen.

And then one voice, one so beloved. "Tara…"

A soft, pulsing warmth seemed to course over her, much as Gavin's hands had touched her on her wedding night. Minutes ago? A lifetime gone?

"Tara…"

The other voices grew louder, stronger, rocking her with their demand that she respond. She didn't know what they wanted. She only wanted to hear that one special voice. His voice.

"Be as one. Let the Exchange begin."

"Tara," he said again, his voice agonized.

Something hot and wet fell upon her face, bathing her in heat and warmth. And the warmth spread in waves along her tired body, waking it, rousing it, infusing it with light and strength.

"Gavin," she tried calling, knowing he was near, but her voice made no sound.

And then she felt his lips upon hers. Warm and soft, tender and possessive. Giving all of himself. Involuntarily, her lips parted and in pure ecstasy, she took him into her mouth. Her love, her husband. Alive, and some-how giving her life.

Not dead, she thought in exultation. He's not dead.

Without warning, time seemed to suddenly focus again. She no longer drifted in a limbo of death's making, but was wholly aware of her body, of the strong arms that surrounded her, of his lips pressed to hers, the wet-ness on both their faces. She raised the hand that still burned and stroked the planes of his wonderful face. And knew him by the feel of his skin, the taste of him, and most of all by the beating of her own heart.

"Be as one now...and for all your days," she heard intoned, more distantly now, as if whoever spoke the words were stepping back, departing.

She opened her eyes as Gavin released her lips.

"Gavin?" she whispered, awed to see him there, stunned by the depth of sorrow etched on his face.

His tear-filled eyes met hers. A broken cry escaped him and he pulled her hard against him, burying his face into her hair. "Oh, God, thank you. Thank you, thank you. You're alive. Oh, my love. You're alive."

She held him as closely as he held her, not sure what had happened, but knowing that some miracle had oc-curred, a miracle that allowed Gavin to have tears, al-lowed herself to draw breath.

After what seemed an eternity, Gavin's shudders sub-sided and he drew back from her a little. She studied him as if she hadn't seen him in a lifetime of searching. And she thought, seeing him now, that it might be true, for this man was a far different one than she'd held earlier. This was a man who had known, lost and rediscovered incredible power.

She stroked his face gently. Lovingly. "I heard people chanting. Where are they?"

"They've gone. They were…friends."

Tara didn't have to guess who they'd been, but asked anyway, "The Council?"

Gavin nodded. "All of them."

"What happened?"

He drew a shaky breath and smiled down at her. "The Exchange," he said. His rich voice was filled with awe.

"What does that mean?" she asked. "To us…"

He shook his head. "I don't know. No one knows. It's never been done before, as far as anyone knows. Just in myth."

"All myths are rooted in some truth," she said.

He smiled crookedly. "All I know is that you are alive. I love you, Tara. I love you with everything that is still good in me."

She smiled up at him lovingly, aching for him. Aching for those years he spent searching for some reason to live. "There is so much good in you, Gavin."

"If there is, it comes from you. You brought it to me."

"You bring me love," she said. "The greatest good there is."

"Forever," he answered. "I'll bring you love forevermore."

"The Exchange is a marriage of sorts, isn't it?" she asked.

He studied her for a long moment, then nodded slowly. "A union of two souls."

"Then…wouldn't you think we deserve a second honeymoon?"

Just as she hoped, Gavin's sorrow and solemnity slowly dissolved and a grin curved his lips even as a blaze of light ignited in his smiling eyes. "Oh, yes, Tara. A lifetime's worth."

His lips fiercely snared hers. And this time, with all that had happened this amazing night of nights, she had no hesitation in returning the kiss of her truly chosen husband.

Chapter 14

Gavin held on to Tara's hand tightly. "Are you frightened?" he asked.

She shook her head, smiling a little at the note of deep tenderness in his voice. She wondered if she was hearing that sentiment more clearly now as a result of the Exchange, or because they loved each other so. She suspected it was a rare combination of both.

Alana stepped forward, resplendent in her black-and-white robe. "Are you ready?" she asked. She sounded far more nervous than either of them.

"We're ready," Gavin said.

"It'll only be a few more minutes," the other woman said, and whirled away, leaving them alone in the small antechamber off the main cavern where the rest of the Council awaited them.

"I love you, Tara," Gavin said. "I don't feel I can ever say it enough."

"That is all I ever want *to* hear," Tara said. "And you know how very much I love you."

"I'll never understand why you do, but I'll never stop being grateful for it, either," Gavin said, drawing her into his arms.

"I think I knew when you first walked into the solarium of the hotel," Tara said.

"And I, when I first heard your laughter." Then, when she would have chuckled, he caught her lips with his and pulled her against him.

In his kiss, she could taste the depth of his love for her, and in his eyes, she could see every dream she'd ever wanted coming true. Strangely, for all the passion, Tara felt composed and serene. In the sharing of their love, in the commingling of their souls, they were joined as they could never have been before.

And yet she did ache for him. For the years he'd spent hating himself, his life, his being.

"Gavin?" she asked, pulling away from him a little. "What will happen to the Council now?"

"They'll learn to change," he said. "As I did. As Jonathan did. And you. They'll have to now, because too many of the Society will want what we've found."

"And is that likely?"

Gavin shook his head. "Miracles don't happen that often."

"And this memorial service today?"

"Is the first step of their changing. A farewell to Jonathan and an apology of sorts. He was a profound lesson for us all."

They both fell silent, contemplating Jonathan's death. And Charlene's. Even, perhaps, Tom's. Without all of them they would not be together now.

"Do you have regrets, Tara?" Gavin asked, sounding suddenly shy.

She shook her head and smiled up at him. "Not when it comes to you, Gavin. Never. I've had no regrets from the first minute you touched me."

"I love you," he said. And there was no smile on his face at all.

"Am I truly one of you now?"

"No, Tara. And neither am I, any longer. We are both more and less."

"What did the myth promise?" she asked, knowing already, but loving to hear him say it again.

"That two souls will mingle in mind and body and share all the elements of both worlds, blending dark with light, day with night, power with vulnerability."

"So we don't know how long we might have together," she said, unconsciously tightening her grip on his arm.

"No one ever knows that," he said. "Just as we don't know about children, about dying, about tomorrows."

"The myth, the Exchange…it's a good definition of love," she said. "So, we're just like any newlywed couple starting out."

"Yes," Gavin agreed, wrapping his arm around her and pulling her as close as it was possible to be. "Strangers one day, partners the next."

"We married for all the wrong reasons," she said.

"And joined for all the right ones."

Alana stepped back into the small antechamber. "They're ready for you," she said, and turned away.

They followed her from the escarpment and moved into the immense cavern.

"Gavin…?" Tara asked, stopping, putting her hand on his to detain him a moment.

He turned, a worried expression on his broad, handsome face. "Yes?"

"I've been practicing. I can fly now. Like you."

As she'd known he would, he first looked shocked then laughed out loud and the echoes of his rich baritone rang throughout the cavern.

* * * * *